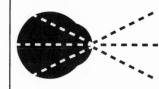

This Large Print Book carries the
Seal of Approval of N.A.V.H.

Panhandle Gold

Kent Conwell

Thorndike Press • Thorndike, Maine

Library of Congress Cataloging in Publication Data:

Conwell, Kent.
  Panhandle gold / Kent Conwell.
    p. cm.
  ISBN 1-56054-571-2 (alk. paper : lg. print)
1. Large type books. I. Title.
[PS3553.O547P36   1992]   92-35421
813'.54—dc20   CIP

All the characters in this book are fictitious, and any resemblance to actual persons, living or dead, is purely coincidental.

Thorndike Large Print® Popular Series edition published in 1992 by arrangement with Avalon Books.

Cover photo by Robert Darby.

The tree indicium is a trademark of Thorndike Press.

This book is printed on acid-free, high opacity paper. ∞

To Gayle, my wife, for her patience and understanding

Chapter One

Anyone who has ever dealt with the common cow will readily swear that the beast by far surpasses all other four-legged animals, and most two-legged, in the race for the title of the most miserable critter the Good Lord ever created. Those slack-jawed bovines are the most onerous animals on the face of the earth.

Boneheaded and stubborn, vexatious and irksome, they're as likely to starve to death in six inches of snow as they are to knock themselves senseless butting up against a tree stump for no good purpose other than it happens to be in their way.

Because cows are so contrary, the main job of a cowpoke on any beef ranch is to keep a constant eye on those dumb creatures to save them from themselves. That was my job, being a cowboy for Joe Eastland on his spread.

I had learned as a youth that cowpunching itself is sheer boredom — sprinkled with moments of stark terror facing a charging bull or being caught up in a stampede.

I never thought I would long for the return of those trying times, but within a few hours after meeting Ben Ross and his spoiled daughter, I found myself wishing I was back out on the range nursemaiding every single one of those knot-headed, cud-chewing bovines.

The day I met Ben Ross, I was searching for strays along a deep arroyo where cattle often wandered to take advantage of the cool shade cast by the vertical walls. Instead of paying attention to my business, I got to dreaming about the ranch I was going to rebuild as soon as I earned enough money to pay off the back mortgage.

I laid out the house, the barn, the pens, and even tried to figure out what a start of purebred stock would cost. When I rode out of that arroyo onto the Texas prairie, I was still daydreaming.

But the boom of an old Henry .44 and the scary *whump* of a two-hundred-grain slug tearing up a chunk of sand in front of my horse brought me back to the present in a hurry. Before the echo died away over the rolling prairie, I had thrown myself from the saddle and pulled my horse to the ground as a makeshift breastwork.

Peering over the rising and falling belly of my chestnut, I squinted into the sun at a wagon sitting cockeyed on the crest of a nearby sand hill. The team stood rigid and alert, necks arched, heads turned, ears pointed in my direction, with only their tails moving to flick at the meddlesome gnats buzzing around their heads. Two other horses were tied to the rear of the wagon, which appeared to have a broken wheel.

Behind the wagon stood two figures, one tall and thickly built, the other small like a woman. I remained where I was, satisfied just to watch for the time being until I could figure out what to do next.

The sun baked down. Heat rose in waves, distorting the horizon. There was no wind. Voices drifted across the prairie. One was a woman's.

Upon hearing the female voice, I decided this was no ambush, so I pulled my bandanna from around my neck and tied it to the muzzle of my pa's Winchester. Waving it over my head, I shouted, "Hold on up there! I'm a friend." I didn't know who that jasper up on the hill was, but I figured the smartest move for me was to claim to be a friend.

After a moment's hesitation, a deep voice called back, "Come on up, but come slow."

Leading my chestnut, I kept my hands high, the reins in my left, the Winchester in my right, its hammer cocked. My finger rested lightly on the trigger. As I drew near, a large man in broadcloth pants and vest stepped around the wagon. He wore brogans instead of riding boots. His sleeves were rolled up

9

to his elbows, and he had slung his coat over the rear seat of the wagon. He held the Henry waist high, centered on me. He was bare-headed, so he had to squint against the sun. "That's far enough. Who are you?"

I stopped at least half a dozen wagon lengths away from him, keeping my eyes on his, waiting for his next move. "Name's Matt Sparks. This here is Eastland range. And I'm asking you the same thing, mister."

A grin broke over his square face. "You're a cocky hombre."

I studied him. He looked about forty-five, maybe fifty. "Nope. It's part of my job to check on anyone coming onto Joe Eastland's land. We've had some missing stock off and on. So I reckon you can see my point."

He lowered his rifle. "You weren't paying much attention to stock when you came out of that gully down there. Looked like you was dreaming about the last church social. And from what I hear back in Antelope Flats, the Kiowa are running wild. That's a bad time to be dreaming."

My ears burned, but I held tight to my temper. I'd found myself too much trouble in the past by giving in to the urge to bust someone up. Before I could reply, he nodded to the slight figure behind the wagon, and a blond-haired girl of about twenty or so, wearing riding pants and a white shirt, stepped out, her eyes on me and a suspicious look on her face.

My ears burned even more when I realized she had been listening as he chided me. I had to say something to regain my pride. "You shoot awful fast on strangers, mister." That was a lame remark, and I realized it as soon as I said it. The funny part was that I didn't know why I said it — at least not for a few days.

He nodded and pointed the muzzle of his Henry at a smart-looking sorrel standing about a quarter of a mile away at the base of a sand hill. For the first time, I noticed a man's body stretched out on the ground. "If I didn't shoot fast, I'd be lying here with a couple of holes in me instead of that bushwhacker yonder. When I saw you, I thought you might be his partner." The big man leaned his brass-frame Henry against a wheel and said, "This is my daughter, Jodie."

Fumbling, I pulled my hat from my head. "Pleased to meet you."

She didn't reply, only looked me up and down as if she were considering buying me. We stared at each other for several seconds. She never said a word.

"I'm Ben Ross," he added, breaking the silence. "And if you don't mind, I can use a hand on this wagon."

I looked away, glad for a chance to turn my attention somewhere else. I'd met unfriendly people before, but she was as unneighborly as a cat in a room full of hounds. I nodded. "Okay, but first we'd better take a look at your bushwhacker. He might still be alive."

"No chance," Ben said, a touch of pride in his voice. "I hit what I aim at. Too bad he didn't know that when he came out of the hills shooting at us."

I went out to check anyway. Ben was right. The man sure was dead. He didn't have any identification on him. I threw the body over the sorrel. In the morning, I'd take him into town.

A movement at the top of a distant sand hill caught my attention. I looked up, but all I saw was a dust devil swirling over the crest of the hill.

Back at the wagon, I saw that half a dozen spokes had snapped in the wheel, throwing the rim. "We can't fix it out here," I said, reaching to untie the two horses at the back of the wagon. "We'll fashion a skid and drag it back to Joe Eastland's place."

"That's my horse," a voice said. Suddenly, the rope was yanked from my hand.

Surprised, I jerked around. Jodie Ross was staring up at me, her eyes defiant. "I'll take care of my own horse, thank you."

"Jodie!"

She snapped back at her father, "It's bad enough I have to come out here to this godforsaken country, but I don't have to put up with some hick cowboy fooling with Blaze, you hear?"

Ben's voice bellowed across the prairie. "You watch what you say, young lady. I'm still your father."

She glared at her father for several seconds in a battle of will. Finally, she dropped her eyes. "Yes, sir."

"You apologize for being so rude."

She stared at me, gritty defiance in her eyes.

"Jolene Sue Ross." The threat in his voice was obvious.

She dropped her gaze back to the ground. "I apologize," she whispered.

At first, I had wanted to snap back, but the words had stuck in my throat. I had never spoken unkindly to a woman, no matter how much she rebuked or criticized me. Now I was glad I hadn't broken a lifelong habit. I shrugged and swung onto my horse, and we struck out for the ranch.

Like all families living in near-isolation across the Texas Panhandle in the 1870s, the Eastlands were bear-hungry for company, so putting up Ben and his daughter for a spell was something in the way of a treat for them.

Joe and Martha Eastland's two children, Mercy and Michael, took to Jodie right away, even though she was five years older than Mercy and six more than Michael. I couldn't help noticing that every time I came near, she looked at me in the same suspicious way Pa had eyeballed his hound when he thought the animal was sucking eggs. Finally, I made it a point to steer clear of her.

The Eastlands' house was whitewashed adobe with a sod roof, the same kind I had on the spread my folks had left me — bank-mortgaged to the hilt, but still mine. The soddy was cool in the summer and warm in the winter, and contrary to what a few skittish folks said, the snakes weren't too bad, especially if the adobe was kept in repair.

The barn out back was built of store-bought lumber, while the corrals and holding pens were fashioned out of wrist-thick and head-high scrub-oak.

The ground around the house and barn was hard-packed both from stock and human traffic as well as always being broom-swept. Prairie fires were a common hazard in the Texas Panhandle, and the simplest way for ranchers to protect their buildings was to eliminate the grass.

After laying out the bushwhacker in the

barn, Ben, Joe Eastland and I worked on the wagon in front of the toolshed. At twenty-nine, I was the youngest of the three, which meant that Ben and Joe could stand back and give instructions while I did most of the hard work. That's when Ben offered me the opportunity I'd been searching for since my folks had been murdered by Indians.

I was heating the rim in the fire when he cleared his throat. He hooked a thumb at Joe. "Joe here says you're looking for a way to make some money for that ranch of yours."

Sweat stung my eyes when I looked up at him. I wiped it out and nodded to the south. I was always eager to talk about my ranch. "Sure would. It's about fifteen miles over that way. It has one of those springs they call artesian at the base of a plateau. Only well like it in the county. Soon as I get a grubstake together, I'm going to pay off the bank note on the mortgage and rebuild the soddy and buy some prime stock."

Ben grinned at Joe. "Joe said you're a hard worker." He paused and the grin faded from his face. "He told me about your folks too. I'm mighty sorry, Matt."

For a moment, my eyes burned, but I ducked my head and fumbled with the rim. "Thanks," I said, probably sounding more gruff than I meant.

Using the hammer and a pair of tongs, I rolled the hot rim onto the wheel. While I hammered the rim down snugly, Ben asked, "Why don't you throw a loop on some of those wild cattle along the Canadian? They're not purebred, but they'd be a start."

Overhead, a flock of geese headed north, honking with every beat of their wings. I looked up at them, probably one of the last flocks of the season. I wasn't surprised. Winter had been long and cold in Texas. There was even a spring snow in late April. I hoped the winter wasn't an omen of what was to come.

"Started to pull some in," I answered. "But unless I was there every day, they'd wander off again. I thought about stringing up some of that barbed wire I've heard about and raising my own herd, but as Joe there will tell you, the ranchers hereabouts don't cotton to wire."

"And probably never will," Joe added.

"What about a bank loan?"

I grinned sheepishly. "Bank says I got no credit because the land is already over-mortgaged."

"Too bad."

"George Wentworth — he's got the ranch to the south of me — well, we've talked some about a loan. I haven't decided. Joe and me have talked about taking off for California and trying to strike it rich."

Ben looked thoughtful. "That's a possibility, but maybe I can help you get by without a loan or having to go to California."

I paused in my work and looked at him curiously.

He said, "I'm here to set up a freight line between Dodge City and Fort Worth. Joe has told me about your being in the war and all. From what I've heard and seen about you, I figure you just might be the man I'm looking for. I'd like to hire you to work for me. What do you know about freighting?"

"I did some bullwhacking up around Oregon and down into California."

Ben beamed. "Good. You're my wagon master as of now. A few years with me, and you'll pay off the land and have herd money left over. I'll even advance you enough to get up to date on your mortgage."

I looked up at him in surprise, one of the few pleasant ones I'd had in the last several months. "You're not joshing me, are you?"

Ben's face broke into a grin. "Not on your life, Matt."

At the moment, he looked like a saint. Naturally, I had been leery about borrowing from Wentworth. I wasn't a fool. I knew that Wentworth wanted my ranch, and by lending me money, he might have the chance to get it if I couldn't repay the debt. I didn't see where I had any choice. I couldn't blame Wentworth — that was just business. But now — I wiped my hand on my denims and stuck it out, then pulled it back.

I hesitated and looked at Joe. "I don't want to put you in a bind, Joe."

Joe shook his head. "That's okay, Matt. Fact is, one of Alton Kincaid's boys was by a few days ago looking for work. It won't be no problem."

"Thanks, Joe. You and Martha have been mighty fine to me. I'm right obliged to you." I stuck out my hand again to Ben. "When do I start?"

"You didn't ask nothing about your wages."

"I've knocked around all over the West, Ben. You strike me as the kind of gent who'll treat me fair."

He pumped my hand. "How does a hundred and twenty-five dollars a month sound?"

At first, I thought I misunderstood. The average cowboy drew only twenty-five to thirty dollars a month. "How much?"

He nodded. "You heard me right. One twenty-five a month. Same as a riverboat captain. I know that's a premium wage, but you'll earn every penny of it. You're traveling with us to Fort Worth as my right-hand man. There's a lot of odds and ends you can attend to. That'll give me time to take care of business."

"Sounds good to me."

"We'll leave first thing in the morning."

"Can't," I said, nodding to the barn where the dead bushwhacker lay. "I've got to haul that man into Antelope Flats tomorrow."

Ross frowned. It was obvious he didn't like to be kept waiting around for anyone. He stared at me as if he were reconsidering his job offer. I hoped he wouldn't, but the dead man, even if he were a bushwhacker, had family somewhere.

Ross nodded to Joe. "Let Joe take him in."

I shook my head. "Not with Kiowa out. He can't go off and leave his family."

"What about Many Dogs?" Joe asked.

Many Dogs was a Kiowa brave I found badly wounded out on the prairie. I took him home, and my ma nursed him back to health. After he returned to his own people, he tried to keep marauding war parties away from our spread, and now from Joe's place, since that's where I lived.

All I could do was shake my head at Joe's question. "We don't know if this is his band or not. I'd hate to chance it, Joe." I paused and looked Ben square in the eye. "I was brought up to be considerate of other people's feelings, Ben. This man's family has a right

19

to know about him. I can sure use that job, but this has to come first."

Ben stared at me with cold eyes.

I figured my job had just flown north with that last flock of geese.

Finally a grin broke Ben's square face. He shrugged. "Why not? Another day won't hurt that much. The animals could do with a rest. It'll give me a chance to check their shoes, and give that spoiled daughter of mine a chance to settle down. She isn't used to Texas travel, or Texas people," he added, winking at me.

I could have turned his last words around and said that Texas people weren't ready for her, either, at least not this Texan. But I kept my mouth closed.

Chapter Two

That night, just before I turned off the lantern in the tack room where I was bunked, there was a knock on my door. "Come on in," I called out over my shoulder as I removed my gun belt and hung it on the wall.

The wood-slab door creaked open. A soft female voice said, "Excuse me."

I spun around and stared at Jodie, who stood just outside the open door. The surprise of seeing her standing there choked back whatever words I might have spoken.

She smiled demurely and dropped her eyes. "I — I just wanted to apologize for being so rude today. It was very unladylike and uncalled for."

A warm feeling rushed through me. "That's all right. I understand."

"It's just —" Her smile gone, she looked up at me, and I saw a sense of futility in her eyes. She gestured outside the barn. "It's just that this country is so —"

I nodded and finished the sentence for her. "Desolate?"

A faint smile curved her lips. "That's about it. But that's no excuse for me to act like I did."

"Like I said, forget it."

Her smile broadened. "Thank you," she said, backing away before turning and heading out of the barn.

I watched as she crossed the ranch yard and disappeared into the soddy. With a shake of my head, I closed the tackroom door and turned off the lantern, surprised but pleased with the turn of events.

That night I dropped off to sleep thinking about Jodie Ross.

The next morning, I loaded the bushwhacker on his horse and took him into Antelope Flats. I got back to the ranch just before dusk the next evening. Ben's wagon sat in front of the barn. I glanced at the corral. One of the horses was missing, but I figured it was feeding in its stall.

Joe hurried out to meet me. His face was serious. "Glad you're back, Matt. We got a problem."

I looked past him. Jodie and Mercy were standing in the doorway watching us, their faces tight with anxiety. Ben was nowhere around.

"Ben Ross just hightailed it to Fort Worth on that big gray of mine. He left Jodie here with us until he gets back. He wants you to catch up with him."

"I don't understand. Why didn't he wait?"

"About an hour after you left this morning, six men rode in to water their animals. Ben and me was in the barn reshoeing his horses. When Ben peeked out the door and saw them, his face went as white as my old pa's beard. Well, I went out to meet them, and Martha brought the men some coffee. While we were standing around the watering trough, one of them said they were heading for Fort Worth."

"A lot of folks go to Fort Worth."

"They was sent to kill Ben Ross, or at least slow him down." He hesitated, then continued. "That's what Ben said. They work for Arnold J. Jordan, a rich businessman from back East. He wants the same freight contract Ben is after. From what Ben says, the contract will make a man rich, and Jordan doesn't want to take any chances on losing it. So he apparently figures to eliminate his competition one way or another."

"What makes Ben think those six are after him?"

"Because the leader of the men was Rafe Cutler. According to Ben, Cutler is Jordan's hired killer. Besides, they looked that wagon over real good. I got the feeling they recognized it."

I turned the situation over in my head. In the last twenty-four hours since I had met Ben Ross, events had sure taken some strange

23

turns. "Do you believe him?"

Joe considered my question. "I think so."

I studied the situation. Over the years, painful experience had taught me to think before taking any action. And this was one of those times. I could see all sorts of problems just waiting to happen, but I believed Ben. He seemed a fair and honest man. I glanced over Joe's head at Jodie and Mercy still standing in the doorway. Remembering Jodie's visit the night before, I glanced at her, but her face remained unsmiling.

I swung down off my horse. "I'll start at first light."

Just then, a cloud of dust billowed on the horizon. I swung back into my saddle and flipped the rawhide loop off the hammer of my gun. Joe reached for his Winchester. A few minutes later, we both relaxed, and I swung down. John Wentworth and his foreman rode in, on their way back home from Antelope Flats.

They watered their horses, and we made small talk. As they started to ride on, Wentworth said, "Remember, Matt, when you need that loan, let me know. All the paperwork is done down at the bank. All you need to do is sign your name." He kept a straight face, but I saw the craftiness gleaming in his eyes.

"Thanks, John, but I won't be needing it."

The smile fled his face. "The bank lent *you* money?"

I didn't answer his question. I just told him again that I didn't need any of his money.

He stared at me hard, as if I had stolen my own ranch from him. "But I've already made arrangements at the bank."

"And I appreciate it, John. But, like I said, I won't be needing the loan."

"Well, now, Mr. Sparks. You turn me down on this after all the trouble and paperwork I've gone to, then don't you ever come hat in hand to me on anything!" Without waiting for an answer, he dug his sharp rowels into his horse's flanks and galloped away.

Joe shook his head and grinned as we walked my horse to the barn. "There's a man that don't like losing."

"Yeah," I replied, realizing that Wentworth wasn't upset over the paperwork at the bank but because he couldn't get his hands on my ranch. "Especially what isn't his."

Jodie and Mercy were still in the door when Joe and I reached the house a few minutes later. I unfastened my gun belt and hung it on the coat pegs just inside the door.

"What are you doing?" Jodie stared up at me with her fists jammed into her hips.

I looked at Joe. He shrugged, just as confused as I was. I turned back to Jodie. "What do you mean?" I nodded to the table. "We're getting ready to eat."

She set her jaw. "My father wants you to catch up with him."

"And I plan on it." I still hadn't figured out what point she was trying to make, but a sneaking suspicion began to nag at me.

"Then why are you taking off your gun? Why aren't you doing what he said?"

There was her point, clear as a new star on the horizon. I shook my head at the ignorance of Easterners and poured water into the porcelain washbasin. "If you're thinking I should follow after him tonight, then somebody juggled your brains around. I plan to leave as soon as I can, which is first thing in the morning. I expect I'll catch him by tomorrow night."

"But that might be too late." Her eyes blazed, and she shook her finger at me. Right there in front of me, the apologetic and humble young lady from last night disappeared, replaced by a pinch-faced, shrewish biddy. "You work for my father. That means you work for me, and I order you to go after him."

My temper snapped. "Then I quit. You go running off blind in the night if you want to, but not me. I'm not rich like you and your pa, but that doesn't mean I'm dumb." I took a step toward her and hooked my thumb over my shoulder. "In case you don't know it, lady, your pa had to swing wide to skirt around that bunch of men. There's no way under the sun I could stumble across him tonight. And even if I could, I don't think I'm much in the mood for it."

I glanced around, suddenly realizing that everyone was staring at me, Martha with surprise, Joe with a grin, Mercy with a look I didn't understand, and Jodie with undisguised hatred. Michael snickered into his milk. I reckon I had said more words in the last minute than I had in the three months I'd worked for the Eastlands.

My ears burned, but I kept my head up. "I apologize, Martha. I didn't mean any kind of reflection on you or yours." I reached for my gun belt and hat. "I'm not really that hungry, so if you folks will excuse me, I'm going to bed down."

As I left for the barn, I heard Joe talking slowly and patiently to Jodie, trying to explain just how futile it would be for anyone to venture out at night. How, in addition to rattlesnakes and Kiowa, the prairie held a thousand other dangers at night even for those who knew what they were doing. Personally, I didn't care if she understood or not. In fact, I would have taken pure delight in seeing her bounced off a horse onto one of those flop-eared cacti that dot the prairie.

By the time I reached the barn, my temper had begun to cool. I lit the coal-oil lantern that swung gently from the rafters. Lost in thought, I stared at the lantern until it stopped swinging. Despite what I had told Jodie, I was still going after Ben.

Maybe I was thinking more of myself, but Ben was the means by which I could rebuild the ranch that my ma and pa and kid sister had been killed over. I wasn't about to pass up that chance. I felt guilty enough about traipsing off to the war back in '64 and then to Arizona afterward, leaving Pa to take care of the ranch. I'd come back from time to time, stay awhile, then leave, the last time in '71.

He refused to let Ma write and tell me how sick he really was, and if I hadn't happened to drop by late in '74, I never would have known he had been ill until it was too late.

And, in truth, '74 was too late. By that time, the bank had a solid mortgage on the ranch, and there was no work where a man could earn enough to pay it off.

Still, Banker Simmons was fair. He gave me a year to catch up on principal and interest. But if I wasn't caught up by then, he would have to sell the place. I was determined that would never happen. So I went to work for

Joe Eastland at fifteen dollars a month, enough to scrape by, but not enough to make any improvements on the ranch or catch up on the mortgage. I kept working and looking, talking to everyone I could about jobs.

I dug into my leather-strapped chest and pulled out Pa's Colt revolver and sat down on my bunk. I removed my own revolver, a Colt '62 Police, from its holster. I studied them both, admiring the blue finish and the oil-stained walnut grips. I much preferred my revolver, but it was a .36 caliber, and Pa's was a 44.40, the same caliber as his Winchester.

He had deliberately purchased both the Winchester and the Colt for that reason. "That way, Matt, in an emergency, the same cartridges can be used in either gun," he had said.

Figuring that could work to my advantage, I cleaned my .36 and stored it in the chest. Then I turned to cleaning Pa's Colt.

Ever since the Kiowa killed my family, I tried to stay busy so as not to think too much about them. But now, with my pa's revolver in my hand, all my memories came flooding back. I tried to think of the good times, but those memories hurt worse than the terrifying sight of the three of them sprawled out and scalped in front of our soddy.

A horse neighed, and I remembered my kid sister, Priscilla. She was sixteen and loved horses. She named every horse on our place, even my chestnut. When she first saw him, she pointed at his stocking feet. "Look, Matt. He looks like he's wearing socks. That's what you should name him — Socks."

Suddenly, the Colt in my hand blurred as tears stung my eyes. I felt as if my whole life were an empty hole.

Early the next morning, the nicker of a horse awakened me. I lay on my bunk, staring into the darkness, trying to figure out what there was about the muffled sound that was different from all the others in the barn. The horse nickered again, and that was when I realized the sound had come from outside the barn.

I threw my legs over the edge of the bed and slipped into my denims and boots. I opened the barn door and stared into the night. Standing at the water trough beside the ranch house was a saddled horse. I strained my eyes against the darkness. The moon slid out from behind a cloud.

My blood ran cold. The horse was the gray that Ben had ridden out on.

Lights came on in the ranch house as I crossed the yard. The gray shifted her feet, but continued to drink. Taking her bridle, I

Ben Ross and his daughter out on the Texas prairie.

After I stabled the gray, I buckled on my gun belt and was pulling on my vest when I heard a faint noise behind me. Mercy Eastland stood staring at me, her blue house robe with the lace around the neck snugged tightly about her. Worry wrinkles lined her forehead.

"You shouldn't be out here," I told her. "It's chilly. You might catch a cold."

A tiny blush colored her cheeks. "I'll be fine. I — I just wanted you to know . . . that is, to tell you to be careful."

I remembered now that Joe had told me that Mercy had a crush on me, but I had paid little attention to his words because of the difference in our ages. I saw now that I had been mistaken. "Don't worry," I said, smiling at her as I slipped a bridle and saddle on Socks. "I'll be just fine. Ben probably just got thrown. I suspect he's hoofing it in now."

I didn't believe that, but there was no sense worrying her any more.

I was tightening the cinch when I felt her hand on my arm. I looked around. Mercy had tears in her eyes. "Hey," I said, touching her cheek. "None of that." I started to tell her that I was too old for her.

"I know what you're thinking, Matt, but fourteen years isn't too much. My aunt was

rubbed her neck. "Easy, girl," I said softly. "Easy."

The mare drank as I slipped my hand onto the saddle. I jerked my hand away and stared at the dark smear on the saddle. I looked at my hand. In the cold moon, the smear on my palm was black, but I knew what it was — blood.

"He's dead. My father's dead, and you killed him!"

I spun around. Jodie stood in the lantern light on the front porch, tears glistening on her cheeks, fists clenched. "He's dead!" she screamed. "And it's all your fault."

Chapter Three

I stared at the blood on my hand and then at the dark smear I had made when I wiped it from the saddle. My stomach churned, and I looked at Joe Eastland, who shook his head. "I was afraid of this," he said.

Martha hurried onto the porch and urged Jodie back into the house, trying to assure the young woman that her father was all right. "Listen to me, child," she said softly. "Matt didn't have any choice. There was no way in heaven he could have found your father last night. But you rest easy. He's a fine man. He'll find your pa."

Her words trailed off as they entered the soddy. I felt sorry for Jodie, for I remembered my own feelings when I found my folks. I knew Martha would make Jodie understand, but I just hoped she wouldn't make any rash promises that I couldn't keep.

A cold moon lit the countryside. I shivered as I stared at the big gray mare. The animal backed away, but I held tight to her bridle, steadying her with my other hand.

I ran my hand down the animal's neck and chest. There was no sweat, which meant the mare, even if she had been driven h earlier, had been walking at her own pace l enough to cool down. I looked to the w "At first light, Joe, I'll backtrack. I'll br Ben back."

Joe nodded. "What do you reckon t place?"

"Who knows? Those jaspers who ca through looking for Ben might have cau; up with him."

He grimaced. "Ben said they were killer

Joe's words sent another cold chill throu my body. "You told me that before. Tl means I'd better not waste any time."

"Okay, Matt. I'll get Martha to start brea fast." He headed for the front door.

"And, Joe —"

He looked around at me just before he we inside.

I nodded toward the house. "Try to ma Jodie understand why I couldn't go after l father last night. That lady and me can't s two words to each other without unsheathi our claws."

"Don't worry, Matt. I'll talk to her."

I nodded. "I'll put up the mare and sad Socks. I'll be only a few minutes." I led t gray through the darkness to the barn, unal to believe just how complicated my life h become in the last thirty-six hours since I n

only fifteen when she married a doctor who was forty."

I didn't know what to say.

She clutched my hand with hers. "Oh, Matt, I'd just die if anything happened to you."

"Nothing will happen," I said. "Believe me."

Mercy tried to smile, but her tears got in her way. "Just promise that you'll be careful."

"I will." I eased my hand from hers. I felt a pang of sympathy for her, and I wished I had time to talk to her, to explain my own feelings. But I didn't have the time, not right now. Our talk would just have to wait until I came back. "Don't worry." I handed her a handkerchief. "Now, dry those tears."

She did, and I mounted Socks. Mercy tagged after me until I reached the house. I looked down from the saddle. "You'd better get dressed."

She gave me a weak smile and went inside.

After a hurried breakfast, Joe and I went outside where we could talk without alarming the others. We both believed the worst had happened to Ben. I swung onto Socks as the sky brightened enough so I could track. Laying my hand on top of my leg, I felt the reassuring tin of matches in my pocket, the one item I considered as essential as my Colt and Winchester.

"You be careful, Matt, you hear?" Joe said.

I grinned as I turned Socks to the west. "Don't you worry, Joe. I got me a ranch to build."

Backtracking the gray's trail was easy, even though I lost the way a few times when it crossed sand. The short grass prairie always firmed again, and within a few minutes I'd see more sign. The trail led to the southwest toward the Red River.

The sun was directly overhead when I spotted circling buzzards on the far side of a small rise. With growing dread, I spurred Socks into a gallop. Beyond the rise, the prairie was black with buzzards. When they saw me, they beat their wings frantically, pushing their lumbering bodies into the air.

With relief, I saw they were feeding on a horse, not Ben. Remaining in the saddle, I studied the ground in a vain effort to piece together what had taken place. I began circling the horse, each time casting out farther. There were plenty of horse tracks, but that was all.

On the edge of a shallow ditch, I jerked Socks to a halt and dismounted. There in the sandy bed were footprints with flat heels — like those on brogans. Ben Ross. Everyone else in this part of the country wore riding boots. The tracks had to be his. Then I saw the bloodstains beside the tracks.

I backtracked and found a crushed section of sagebrush and dark stains on the sand. Apparently, he had fallen from the saddle when he was shot.

Turning back, I followed his footprints to where he had remounted the gray. The lengthening tracks indicated that perhaps his wounds were superficial. He had spurred the gray into a gallop, a gait that demanded precise physical coordination on the rider's part in order to maintain rhythm with the animal. His trail indicated that he was heading directly for the river. I followed, hoping that my deduction was right. But I could not rid myself of the nagging worry that I was trying to fool myself.

Just before reaching the river, I found where Ben had fallen out of the saddle. What had happened then was easy to read. The gray spooked and headed back to the ranch, leaving Ben on foot.

I followed Ben's zigzagging trail through the sagebrush to the Red River, a broad, sandy bed half a mile wide with a tiny stream meandering down its middle. Red sandstone bluffs lined the north bank of the river. That's where I lost the trail, among the bluffs.

The blood-colored bluffs along the river reminded me of a row of puffy clouds, their crowns round and smooth. Below, the bluffs were honeycombed with caves. Despite the gritty texture of the stone, the footing was treacherous, especially for a horse in steel shoes like Socks. Whenever I wanted to look over the edge of the bluffs, I dismounted and went on foot.

The remainder of the afternoon I spent riding up and down the Red, searching the numerous caves, hoping to run onto a stray track in the moist sand along the sagebrush-dotted shore that would show me the direction Ben had taken. But I found nothing. It was as if the ground had opened up and swallowed him.

The setting sun painted the clouds pink and gold, illuminating the countryside with a warm, orange glow as I searched for a cave in which to spend the night. Just before dark, I found one in the back of a brush-filled hollow, a cave large enough to picket Socks while I spent the night roaming the top of the bluffs, hoping to spot Ben's fire.

With only starlight to see the treacherous bluffs by, I moved slowly, making sure each foothold was solid as I clambered up and down the weather-smoothed sandstone. Finally, a waning moon rose, making travel easier. I glanced at the Big Dipper. Midnight.

Two hours later, I spotted a fire across the river and about a mile downstream. I muttered an oath. I had crossed the Red River only once, but that one time the experience had more than exceeded every warning I had ever been given about the river.

Twisting its way down the sandy bed, the narrow stream of water constantly shifted back and forth. The stream could cut through the sand on the south side one morning; the next it would move north, leaving behind deadly pockets of quicksand. A careful man faced no threat from the sand, but one in a hurry or unheedful of his steps could sink up to his waist within seconds.

After reaching the base of the bluffs, I cut straight across the river, testing every step before placing weight on my foot. Thirty minutes later, after much backtracking and zigzagging, I reached the south shore and cut east. The sage and short grass of the prairie would make easier traveling, but I opted to stay in the willow brakes. Night on the Texas prairie is cool, and that's when the rattlesnake hunts. And I wasn't eager to be its prey.

Within an hour, I sat crouched in a tangle of willow roots, studying the small campfire. The cool night air chilled the sweat on my forehead, and the steady serenade of crickets provided a background for the occasional shriek of a rabbit caught up in the talons of a swooping hawk, or the sudden scrabbling of mice feet over sand and leaves to escape a marauding snake.

Only four men slept around the fire. If this was Cutler's bunch, that meant two were missing. One was certainly on guard. That left one to account for.

The hair on the back of my neck prickled. Wrapping my fingers around the walnut grip of my Colt, I held my breath. The night sounds continued, but I forced them aside as I strained for any alien sound beneath the soft buzz of the creatures of the dark.

The ice-cold click of a hammer being cocked froze me.

A slurred voice said, "Do not move, señor. I do not wish to shoot you."

"Don't worry, amigo," I said, trying to still the pounding in my chest. "I don't wish that, either."

"Very slow now, señor, if you please. Hands over your head. Go to the fire."

Just before we reached the fire, he whistled, and each man rose from his bedroll to his feet, gun in hand. One of the men stepped forward. He was built like a rock, and the firelight reflected off eyes cold as granite.

I had just met up with Rafe Cutler.

The vaquero who had found me said, "He was watching the camp."

Cutler nodded to the fire, and one of the men fed it kindling. Cutler looked at me and snarled, "What are you up to? You some kind of lawman?"

"Not me, mister," I said, knowing my only chance was to play my bluff to the hilt. "My horse busted a leg a couple of days back. I've been on foot since. Hid my saddle early this morning. I spotted your fire, but I wanted to make sure I was welcome. I'm not from around here, and I sure didn't come here looking for trouble."

Cutler studied me with those cold eyes. I kept my own fastened on his. He struck me as the kind to figure a man was a weakling if he didn't look him in the eyes. After a moment, he nodded at one of the vaqueros, who quickly searched me.

The man pulled out my wallet, opened it, then jammed it back in my pocket. "The gringo has nothing, Señor Cutler." With a deft move, he took my .44 out of my hand and tossed it to Cutler.

Cutler relaxed, but still kept his gun trained on me. "What happened to your grub?" he asked, noting that I came into camp empty-handed.

I cleared my throat. "I reckon you could say I left Fort Bascom on the spur of the moment. Not even time to pick up my war bag."

Cutler's eyes glittered. "Maybe you're what you say you are, and maybe you ain't. Get over by the fire where we can watch you."

41

He turned to the vaquero who had captured me. "Backtrack. See what you can find."

With a brief nod, the man disappeared into the night. I didn't have anything to worry about from him. Even if he tracked me across the river, no one can track over sandstone.

"How about some coffee?" I asked, squatting by the fire.

Cutler nodded. "Give him some, Billy Wayne."

A young boy of about eighteen poured some in a battered tin cup and handed it to me.

"Thanks," I said, taking the cup.

While I sipped the coffee, the others squatted around the fire. Cutler remained standing and stuck my .44 in his waistband. "Man can get himself shot dead out on the prairie at night," he said.

"Reckon you're right, mister. I'm much obliged for the coffee and the fire. I can't say I blame you for being cautious of a jasper who just wanders in from the night, but I guarantee I'm no threat to anyone. I'm just trying to reach Fort Sill."

"What's there?" He was still suspicious.

I shrugged. "Horses and work."

His eyes grew wary. "There's a town about forty miles north by the name of Antelope Flats. Why didn't you head that direction?"

"A real town with work?" He nodded. I

continued, "I told you, mister, I'm not from around here. Why, I didn't even know that town was up there. But if it is, I reckon it's a lot closer than Fort Sill, so that's where I'll head come morning." I hesitated, then decided to add a little flair to my bluff. "As you know, I'm flat busted, but if you could see your way clear to lend me a horse, I'll send you the money at whatever post office you name."

Cutler's sneer faded. He spun his revolver on his finger and slapped it back in its holster. He grinned, or at least that's what he intended to do, but it was more like a wolf baring his fangs. He squatted across the fire from me.

He introduced himself and the others. The boy, Billy Wayne, nodded, but the vaqueros didn't even flinch. They just kept their cold eyes fastened on me. "We're headed to Fort Worth," Cutler said. "Got no animals to spare, so I reckon Antelope Flats is your best bet."

"Thanks. By the way, I don't reckon you got a plate of grub about? I haven't eaten all day." Another lie, but part of my bluff.

He glanced at Billy Wayne. "Toss him some jerky."

Before Billy Wayne could move, a horse rode up in the darkness. As one, Cutler and his men jumped to their feet and reached for their guns. A voice called from the night, "It's only me."

43

Billy Wayne grinned at me as if to say everything was all right. "It's Two-Bit."

I picked up the coffeepot and moved to the other side of the fire. I didn't know who this Two-Bit was, but I had the feeling that my luck had already stretched just about as far as it could without breaking.

Cutler yelled at the newcomer. "It's about time. You find Ross? We've —"

Two-Bit stopped at the edge of the firelight and stared at me, frowning. I had never seen him before, but he acted like he knew me. I poured some coffee.

The frown on his face disappeared. "I know him," he said, pointing a finger at me while his other hand streaked for his gun. "That's the guy who helped Ben Ross and his kid back near Antelope Flats."

Chapter Four

I reacted instantly. I threw the scalding coffee at the men and kicked at the fire, spraying burning coals on them. The firelight reflected off the .44 in Cutler's waistband. As my right fist smashed against his jaw, I ripped the revolver from his belt with my left.

The next instant, I leaped into the darkness. At least I knew Rafe Cutler hadn't found Ben yet, but that didn't mean that the businessman wasn't lying dead on the prairie, either.

Moments later, Cutler's voice echoed through the night. "Kill him. You hear me — find him and kill him."

I ran in a crouch across the prairie, zigzagging around the sage and lifting my boots high in an effort to avoid the rattlesnakes. The voices behind me separated. After several hundred yards, I cut back to the river, hoping I could find where I had crossed earlier.

Just as I reached the willow brakes, a dark figure in a large sombrero shot out of the shadows in front of me. The starlight reflected off the knife in his raised hand. Without slackening my speed, I threw myself at him. My hand shot out, and I wrapped my fingers around his wrist as my momentum slammed us into the tangle of roots at the base of the willows.

He grunted and weakened for a moment, but before I could take advantage of his momentary lapse, he tore his hand from my fingers and slashed at me. I lunged forward, cracking my shoulder against his forearm and driving it into the ground.

The knife sawed at my shoulder as I straddled him, but I felt no pain, only a great pressure. I grabbed his wrist with both hands and tried to tear the knife from his grasp. With his free hand, the vaquero beat on my shoulders and head.

With a vicious grunt, I ripped the knife from his hand, sending it flying into the sandy riverbed. Then I slammed a left into the side of his head. For a moment, he went limp.

I leaped for his knife. Just as I wrapped my fingers around the handle, he landed on my back with his knees, driving the breath from me. His clawed fingers dug into my eyes and pulled my head back, bending my neck so much I thought it would snap. I could hear myself groaning.

Awkwardly, I slashed back over my head. The knife hit bone. He screamed. With a sharp twist, I scooted from under him and jumped to my feet. He grabbed for his revolver. I was no expert with a knife, but I threw the double-edged blade at him, hoping to distract him long enough so I could pull out my own gun.

The vaquero froze, stiffened, then grabbed at his chest. The knife handle protruded from his chest.

He sank to his knees while I watched in horror. I had killed him. He was not the first man I had ever fought, but he was the first that I had killed — or at least the first I knew I had killed.

During the war we had killed, but firing at bluecoats across a battle-ravaged field and striking down an unknown soldier was not the same as standing toe-to-toe with an enemy and watching him die. Frozen by the sudden turn of events, I stared at the dead body before me. I heard a groan at my shoulder. I spun around.

There stood Billy Wayne, his eyes fixed on the dead vaquero. The hand holding his revolver had dropped to his side. He had been stunned by the vaquero's death even more than I. I grabbed his gun hand and cracked the muzzle of my own revolver against his temple. He dropped like a pole-axed ox.

That left four men, still too many to fight. I fled back across the river, the dying man's face in front of me. Just before sunup, I reached the cave. I forced the vaquero from my mind. After building a small fire using sagebrush, I set up a few alarms just in case they stumbled into the cave. Then I tended the cut on my shoulder.

The wound was superficial, for the vaquero had been unable to gain the leverage to make a deep cut because his forearm was pinned into the sand. Afterward, I gave Socks some grain and some water from my canteen.

I had planned on watering him at the river, but with Cutler's bunch around, I couldn't chance their stumbling over our tracks. And when I started looking about for Ben's sign later on in the day, I'd have to be doubly careful, with one eye on the ground and one eye on the horizon.

I dug out a pack of jerky and twisted off a chunk with my teeth. I had no appetite, but my body needed sustenance. When my folks had put up drifters, I had heard tales more than once of how the Texas weather could dry all the juices in a body before you were even aware of it. The next thing you knew, you were dead. "Even if you ain't hungry," one old man drawled, "you got to force yourself to eat. Your body needs the energy to keep on."

So I forced myself to eat, but the more I chewed on the jerky, the bigger it got, like a mouthful of cotton. Even water didn't help.

I knew what the cause was, but there was nothing I could do about it. I managed to choke down a few bites.

I must have dozed off, for when I looked around, the cave was dark except for a few winking coals, and I had a bad crick in my neck. Outside, the sun was directly overhead. Time to do a little scouting.

The sandstone bluffs were hot to the touch, but I crawled over them like a snake, staying in the crevices and low spots so I wouldn't present any kind of silhouette. A body standing on a bluff like that can be spotted for miles.

Far to the south, a hawk circled lazily on the rising air currents. After a spell, I decided to push on. From the way he pranced around, Socks was feeling spry. I would search a few more hours for Ben, then head back to the ranch and rest up for a longer search.

I didn't have any luck. Once or twice during the afternoon, I spotted some of Cutler's band and hid in nearby arroyos before they saw me. In the late afternoon, I turned Socks north.

It was dark when I reached the Eastlands' ranch. I put up Socks and headed for the house. The door burst open and Mercy came running out. "Oh, Matt, you're back!" She threw her arms around my neck and hugged me.

My ears burned as I awkwardly returned her hug.

Martha came to my rescue. "Mercy, let the man go. I reckon he's a mite hungry."

Mercy let go, but she tagged after me into the house and sat right beside me at the table while I ate and told them what had taken place. I hesitated, then decided not to say anything about Ben's being shot or the bloodstains in the sand.

Jodie was strangely silent when I finished, but I could tell by the expression on her face that she was worried and upset. "You're sure he's okay?"

"He isn't dead, or I would have found him. And I know for a fact Cutler doesn't have him. So you just rest easy. He's probably holed up in one of those caves, and it's just a matter of time until I find him," I replied.

I looked at Joe, who knitted his brows. "So I figured that I would stock up on grub and spend whatever time it takes to run Ben down," I added.

Joe shook his head. "Just you be careful. This morning Many Dogs was waiting for me down by the south pond. He told me that Lone Wolf and Sky Walker have gone blood-crazy and are leading a band of Kiowa against local ranches. He said he would try to keep them away from here, but he can't promise they'll listen to him."

"Then I'll go with you," a woman's voice said.

It was Jodie. She had a determined look on her face.

I started to laugh, but when I saw just how serious she was, I hesitated. I shook my head. "No. It's too dangerous out there."

"I can take care of myself." Her eyes threw knives at me. "Don't think I can't."

I stared at her, wishing she would grow up. Where I was heading wasn't going to be an easy trip. "I don't care — you're not going. I got all I can do out there to take care of myself."

"You can't stop me."

"I'll stop you even if I have to hog-tie you. Cutler has four men. If he's after your pa, then you'd make a right nice prize for him. You'd best stay here with the Eastlands."

She glared at me.

Joe spoke up. "Matt's right, Jodie. He'll find your pa. You stay here where it's safe."

I expected her to explode like a green horse with its first saddle cinched on, but to my surprise the set look disappeared from her face and she nodded. "I suppose you're right, Matt. It's just that I want to do all I can to help."

Her meek acceptance surprised me. Maybe

51

I was wrong; maybe she was growing up. But whatever caused her to change was fine with me. "Don't worry," I said. "I'll find your pa. I got a feeling he's hiding out in one of the caves along the Red." I looked at Joe. "I'll light out first thing in the morning."

Jodie smiled and said, "I'm sorry I've been so hard to get along with. It's just that my father is all I have left in the world. I'd die if anything happened to him."

I shook my head emphatically, hoping to remove some of the hurt she felt. "Nothing will. Believe me."

"I hope you're right."

Martha patted Jodie's hand. "He is." Then she rose and wiped her hands on her apron as she looked at me. "You'll need a good supply of solid food." She shot a look at Mercy. "Come on in the kitchen and help me put some food together for Matt."

Mercy frowned, and her mother gave an exasperated sigh. "Matt will be here when you finish."

Jodie looked at me from across the table. "You said something about caves along the river."

"That's right. The bluffs along the north bank of the Red are honeycombed with caves. That's where I figure your pa is hiding out." For her sake, I tried to sound confident.

She rested her elbows on the table and leaned forward. "Won't Cutler figure the same thing?"

"He might, but your pa should be able to outfox him. From what I've heard, those caves are all linked together so they can't trap him in any one place."

Joe chimed in, "That's the gospel. I came to the Panhandle when I was just a button. There were a lot of stories of how tribes of old-time Indians lived in them caves and made arrowheads out of pure gold. One such story even claimed there was a room chock-full of golden ingots just waiting for someone to discover."

Jodie laughed. "Golden ingots? You're making that up."

"No, ma'am," he said. "Story is that some robbers used the caves to hide what they stole, that they'd drive their wagons right inside the caves. There was even talk of a wagon train of gold being hid out in the caves. 'Course, nobody's ever seen none. That was just the story, but I don't reckon there's a solitary soul who's grown up around here who hasn't poked around those caves just out of curiosity. When I was a young man, four or five of us explored some of the caves. Like I said, we didn't find no gold, but what Matt said is true. Most of them caves are all hooked together like a big spiderweb."

Jodie looked at me. "And you think my father will be all right?"

I tried to sound confident. "I sure do."

She brushed her blond hair from her eyes and smiled, and I figured that she was satisfied that we were doing all we could.

"Have you ever been out to the caves before now?"

"Once or twice," I answered, relaxing now that the conversation had taken a turn away from argument.

She asked one or two more questions about the caves, then leaned across the table and laid her hand on mine. "Thank you, Matt."

Her hand felt soft and warm. "For what?" I managed to choke out.

"For helping my father and me."

My ears burned. "That's okay. I like your father." No sooner had I spoken than I realized how it must have sounded. I started to add that I liked her too, but she rose and said, "Now, if you men will excuse me, it's time for me to go to bed."

Joe grinned at me as Jodie left the room. "I guess she's decided to let us handle it."

"Yep," I answered, rising and stretching my arms over my head. "It does look that way. Now, tell me what Many Dogs had to say about the Kiowa." We talked for another half hour before I turned in.

At four o'clock the next morning, Joe shook me awake. "Matt! Wake up! Jodie's run off after her pa!"

Chapter Five

While I saddled Socks and lashed my gear behind the cantle, Joe scoured the ground around the corral by lantern light. Finally, he found her tracks, or the tracks we thought to be hers. She had headed due south for the Red. Despite my impatience, I knew that I had to wait for the sun for the same reason I didn't take out after her pa three nights earlier — not even an Indian can track at night.

Jodie might have left the ranch heading due south, but the initial direction means nothing when you track a tenderfoot. She could cut due east or west at any time, for any or no reason, and I would ride right past her sign. And there was always the chance her horse might have stepped in a hole and thrown her. A limp body lying among the sage would be next to impossible to spot, even with the light from the stars and moon.

"How big a start do you reckon she has on us?" I asked.

Joe shrugged. "Her bed ain't been touched. She must have left us in the kitchen last night, climbed out the window, and while you and me talked about the Kiowa, saddled her horse and rode out."

Muttering a few dark oaths about her having riverside clay for brains, I stared at the eastern horizon, trying to will the sun to rise. Martha came out and insisted I eat breakfast. "You can't go nowhere until you can see to follow her tracks, Matt."

She was right. I went inside and ate, but the food tasted like cardboard.

At false dawn, when it was still impossible to find her tracks other than with a lantern, I was sitting in the saddle down at the corral. Joe squatted and directed the glow of the lantern on a U-shaped print. He ran his finger around the perimeter of the mark. Unfortunately, there was nothing unusual about the tracks, nothing to distinguish them from another set or from any of a thousand others.

I said nothing, but when I looked at Joe, I knew that he was thinking the same thing I was. If I ever lost her trail, it would be almost impossible to pick it up again.

"Track slow," he said.

To the east, the first traces of false dawn trudged over the horizon, slowly pulling a blanket of orange after it. I moved out slowly, for the tracks were still difficult to discern. But as the sky lightened, I rode faster.

My head never stopped turning, and my eyes never stopped searching the prairie around me. Kiowa were right sneaky in their ambushes. They could hide in a clear patch of land and jump a man when he rode by.

A knot of apprehension churned in my stomach. The job of saving Ben from Cutler and his killers was dangerous enough, but now the Kiowa had gone blood-crazy, scalping and murdering, and to top it all off, I was saddled with a foolish, stubborn woman who had deliberately ridden right into the middle of the whole mess.

Pa jumped into my head, and I wondered what he would do in my shoes. Just as fast, I pushed him out. I couldn't afford to get caught up in any kind of grief out on the prairie. Those who have been out there on the Texas plains can tell you that a landscape that looks harmless as a newborn kitten one second can turn into a snarling mountain lion the next.

At that moment, I wished I was back punching beef, putting up with ornery cows and chasing down skittish calves. I even wouldn't have minded slopping grease on their ringworms.

At noon I pulled up and scanned the horizon before me. I had no idea how much time I had made up on Jodie, if, indeed, I had made up any. From the sign, she must have kept Blaze in a walking gallop. I clicked my tongue, and Socks broke into a gallop. For the next two hours, I pushed him hard.

At midafternoon, I stopped at the base of a sand hill to breathe Socks. Ground-reining him, I slipped to the top of the hill to see what was ahead. The way I figured it, the Red was only a couple of miles farther.

A flush of elation swept over me. Jodie was less than a quarter of a mile ahead. I stood up to yell, but dropped to my knees as fast as I could. A couple of miles to the east was a band of Indians. The only reason they hadn't spotted Jodie was that two sand hills stood between them.

Within seconds, I leaped into the saddle, jerked Socks around, and dug my heels into his flanks, sending him flying around the base of the hill. I crossed my fingers, knowing that when I rode out onto the prairie, I would be in plain sight for several seconds until I gained the shelter of the next hill.

I reached it without any sign that the Indians had spotted me. About that time, Jodie looked around, surprise on her face. She wheeled her horse, but before he could reach full stride, I caught her.

Knowing we had no time to spare, I grabbed her reins and angled toward a deep arroyo to our right.

"What do you think you're doing?" she

yelled into the wind.

I glanced over my shoulder. She was clutching the saddle horn with both hands as we sped across the prairie. Her face was a mask of anger. She yelled something else, but the wind blew her words away. I looked past her. The Indians were still behind the last sand hill. To the south, the rounded bluffs lining the Red River protruded out of the prairie, but they were too far to reach before the Indians saw us.

The twisting arroyo was deep and narrow, its sandy walls cut by shallow ditches carrying runoff from the infrequent but heavy prairie rains. We rode down into the arroyo and cut south toward the river.

Jodie gripped the saddle horn tightly. Her hat had blown off and was bouncing against her back, held on by a string. Her hair looked like a yellow tumbleweed.

I pulled up around a bend. Before she could yell, I jumped from the saddle and raced up a runoff ditch so I could peer over the rim of the arroyo.

"Are you crazy? I —"

I spun around and threw her a threatening look. "Shut up if you want to keep your scalp." My words came out in a hiss. She must have believed me, for she clamped her lips shut and stared at me.

Turning back, I watched the Indians draw closer. They were Kiowa. Their braided hair fell on either side of their heads, just like Many Dogs'. He had once told me that braided hair was less likely to cause problems in battle than unbraided. I didn't have any reason to disbelieve him.

I heard Jodie crawling up beside me. She stopped when her shoulder touched mine. Without a word, I pointed at the Kiowa. They were headed directly for us.

She caught her breath and looked around at me.

I returned her look and nodded, surprised that I should also notice how clean she smelled. Fresh, with a touch of some kind of perfume.

"What do we do?" Her voice shook, but there was a set to her jaw that I liked. I saw the determination in her eyes as I nodded toward the Red.

"This arroyo leads to the river. We'll follow it and hide in one of the caves until the Kiowa are gone."

She looked down at our horses. "What about tracks?"

I saw what she meant. There was the S shape of snake bellies, sticklike bird tracks, and pug marks of coyotes and wolves in the smooth sand. Horse tracks in the arroyo bed would stand out like a red barn in the middle of a prairie.

"What's our choice?"

Jodie looked me square in the eyes. "None."

We mounted and headed for the river.

Fifteen minutes later, we reached the Red. On both sides, willow brakes abutted a sandstone plate that stretched half a mile along the entrances to the caves on either side of the arroyo. Sagebrush lined the willow brakes.

"There," I said, leading the way. I pointed to the sandstone plate ahead of us. Sand had washed and blown into depressions in the plate. "Stay out of the sand. We don't want to leave any sign."

We passed up several caves until we found one that made a sharp turn just inside the entrance. Jodie's horse, Blaze, stumbled at the entrance, caught himself, then clattered on inside. Dismounting, I led the horses around the bend and put the reins in Jodie's hands. "You wait here. I'll be back."

I expected her to protest, but she nodded and remained silent. I checked outside the entrance to the cave, making sure there was no sign to indicate our passage. Just inside, I saw where Blaze had scarred the sandstone when he stumbled. The scar was small but obviously fresh.

I dragged my fingers over my sweaty forehead and rubbed the moisture into the scar, hoping to dull it. Suddenly a horse whinnied off to my left. Without taking time to look around, I leaped back inside the cave.

I peered from around the corner of the cave just as the band of Kiowa rode out of the arroyo. After some gesticulating, the band split. Half rode west, the other half east in our direction. I hurried back to Jodie.

She listened as I explained our situation. Without a word, she slipped her saddle rifle from its case and levered a cartridge in the chamber. I smiled at her, then pulled my own gun.

Outside, unshod hooves clattered on the sandstone, grew silent, then continued again. In my mind's eye, I watched the Kiowa pull up in front of each cave, peer inside from atop their ponies, then ride on. A few minutes later, they pulled up in front of our cave. We peered around the corner, knowing they couldn't see us back in the darkness of the cave.

I gripped my revolver tighter when I saw the paint on their horses.

The Kiowa rode on. Suddenly, the last one pulled up and slid off his pony. He knelt by the scarred stone at the entrance. After studying it a few seconds, he stared back into the darkness.

I tightened my finger on the trigger.

A guttural voice called out to the Kiowa. He shook his head and remounted his pony. The voice called again, and the warrior shook his head again and rode away.

I breathed easier.

After they rode on, I whispered to Jodie, "We got to hightail it out of here. The Kiowa are painted for war, and this time they won't quit for anyone."

"How do you know that?"

"Their horses. They're painted with hailstones."

"Hailstones?"

"Yeah. They believe if they paint hailstones on their mounts, the ponies become invisible, and since they're riding the ponies, they also become invisible. That's why when they attack they don't stop, because they figure no one can see them."

Under her breath, she whispered, "Oh."

We sat silently in the darkness of the cave, waiting for the Kiowa to distance themselves from us. Jodie broke the silence. "I hate Indians." She paused, waiting for me to reply. When I didn't, she asked, "Well, don't you?"

"Some. Some are not bad, just like white folks."

"I don't know how you can say that. Not after what they did to your —" She broke off. "I mean . . ."

Her words brought back memories. "Yes," I answered, "even after they killed my family. Best we could piece together, the ones responsible for killing my folks were Comanche, some of the Kawadi left over from Quanah Parker's bunch of renegade Indians."

"They're all savages as far as I'm concerned." Her tone was smug and rank with conceit.

Not that I figured I'd change her mind, but I told her about Many Dogs, the Kiowa warrior whose life I had saved. "He is the grandson of Sitting Bear, who was killed back in '71. Like his grandfather, Many Dogs is a member of the Kiowa Kaitsenko, the Society of the Ten Bravest. He is as honorable and trustworthy as any white man — more than most as far as I'm concerned."

She gave a sarcastic laugh. "I've never heard of any Indian being honorable or trustworthy."

"No?"

"No."

"What about that last warrior, the one who got down off his pony to look into the cave?"

"What about him?" Her words were clipped.

"Why didn't he give the alarm?"

"He didn't see us, that's why."

I chuckled. "He saw us, all right. Didn't

you see the grin on his face?"

"All right then, you tell me. Why didn't he give the alarm?"

"That warrior was the friend I was telling you about. That was Many Dogs."

For one of the few times since I had known her, Jodie Ross couldn't think of a smart reply.

We waited until the sun touched the western horizon, balancing like an orange ball on a black string. Then we mounted and rode out of the cave and cut west, heading for the arroyo. Just as we rode past the next cave, a horse shot out and slammed into mine. Out of the corner of my eye, I saw Jodie's pinto rear on its back legs.

Knife in hand, a Kiowa screamed and hurled himself from his pony. I threw myself against the neck of my horse, and the Kiowa flew over me and slammed onto the sandstone at our feet.

I rolled off the horse and pulled my own knife just as the Kiowa leaped to his feet and faked a lunge at me. I jumped back, then we circled, each watching the other warily. He had the advantage, for there were other Kiowa around and surely some had heard his cry. I had to end the fight fast before they arrived.

He lunged and slashed. I parried, but he was a more skillful fighter and the tip of his blade nicked the back of my hand. Suddenly he made a sweeping slash that would have sliced me rib to rib. I parried again, but in the next breath, he hooked his blade against the spine of my knife and gave a sharp jerk.

My knife skittered across the sandstone.

He gave a victory cry and threw his muscle-corded body at me. I grabbed his wrist with my left hand, and with my right I smashed him between the eyes. He staggered. Before he could react, I hit him again, this time directly on the bridge of his nose.

While he was still stunned from my blows, I seized his wrist with my other hand and twisted his arm back until the knife fell to the ground. He was beating on my back, but to no avail. Fisticuffs don't come naturally to an Indian, so now I had the advantage.

I spun him around and let loose a left hook into his jaw. His legs buckled, and he stumbled back. I got overconfident and waded into him. Indians might not know how to fight like the white man, but they can kick, which is what he did, a looping kick from the ground up that grazed my chin and sent me reeling backward.

He leaped for his knife. I was right after him, pushing my knees into the small of his back. He grunted, and I drove a fist into his temple. Abruptly, he went limp.

I tore his knife from his lifeless fingers and

jerked it over my head. Blood pounded in my ears. I hesitated, remembering the vaquero I had killed only a couple of days earlier. My anger cooled. Slowly, I lowered the knife.

When I looked around, Jodie was staring at me, her eyes wide with horror, her face white with shock. I turned the warrior over and put my hand on his chest. He was still breathing.

"W-what are you going to do?" Her voice shook with the disbelief of what her eyes had just witnessed.

I rose and retrieved my own knife. I took a deep breath to still the shaking in my muscles. Suddenly, I froze.

"The horses! Where are our horses?"

Jodie continued to stare with glazed eyes at the inert Kiowa.

I grabbed her shoulders and shook her. "Did you hear me? What happened to the horses?"

Understanding came back into her eyes. She looked around in alarm, frantically trying to grapple with the confusing events that had occurred in the last several seconds. "I — They were here, just a minute ago. They . . ." Her voice trailed off.

The sound of hoofbeats downriver was all I needed to hear. I glanced over my shoulder. The lower third of the blood-red sun had slipped below the horizon. For Jodie and me, that was a stroke of luck, which had favored us so far except for the lone Kiowa. For the moment, the willow brake hid us from the oncoming Indians.

The caves were the only choice we had. "Let's go," I said, pausing to rip several branches from a sagebrush for torches. Jodie didn't argue.

Behind the first bend in the cave, I struck a match to one of the sage branches. Sage burns fast, and, wet or green, ignites almost as fast as dry wood. The torch gave off a small glow, enough to make our way around a bend and deeper into the cave. The clatter of hooves from outside echoed down the cave.

"Hurry," I whispered, straining my eyes against the gloom. I felt her hand on my belt. Suddenly I stopped. Jodie ran into me.

"What's the matter?" she asked.

I extended the flickering torch. The weak glow of the torch fell into a bottomless pit in the middle of the cave floor. Jodie sucked in her breath and dug her fingers into my arm. Neither of us spoke as I ran the torch around the perimeter of the hole. There was a narrow passage on one side.

From behind came the sound of running feet. Pressing against the wall, we edged by the hole, then turned back down the cave, moving as quickly as we could. The padding of moccasins grew louder.

Suddenly, screams rent the air.

"Did they —" Jodie was unable to complete her sentence.

"Sounds like it. We'd better hurry. The others will soon find their way around the hole."

The trail in the cave twisted and turned, sometimes up, sometimes down. We came to several forks. Just to maintain some kind of direction, I always took the left fork. We kept our eyes on the floor. Somewhere along the way, Jodie slipped her hand into mine.

That was when I realized why I had made that lame remark to her father out on the prairie when I first met them. I had immediately liked Jodie and had wanted her to like me. I squeezed her hand, and to my delight she tightened her grip. I glanced over my shoulder.

If the Kiowa were still following, they hadn't gained on us. Maybe we did have a chance. We paused while I lit another branch, then we continued.

Abruptly, the cave ended.

"What —" I ran the torch along the wall, but there was no passage. I swallowed hard as I held the torch between us so we could see each other. "Back," I said. "We have to go back."

"But where?"

"I don't know. Back to the last fork."

"Perhaps we should just stay here," Jodie said in a frightened voice. "They might have stopped following us."

I squeezed her hand. "Maybe, but we can't afford to take that chance. If they catch us here —" I left unspoken the rest of my thought, but her hand tightening on mine told me she understood.

Quickly, I led us back to the last fork. Before we turned into the new passage, we stopped and listened. The silence lay heavy. The weak torch flickered dimly, casting disconcerting shadows across Jodie's face. Then we heard it. A slight scraping sound.

As one, we turned down the passage, which cut sharply to the right after several feet. Just past the turn, our torch suddenly flared, the flame licking at the wall on our left. I paused and held out the torch. There was a recess in the wall that appeared to be about ten feet deep and just as wide. It looked as if it had been deliberately cut, for the sides of the niche were smoother than the surrounding walls of the passage.

It reminded me of the alcove back in Martha's house where she had set her china cabinet. Just as I started to turn away, I noticed a shadow on the back wall where there shouldn't have been one. I stepped into the alcove and discovered a passage in the back corner of the recess.

About as wide as a single tree, the passage went straight into the side wall for only a couple of feet, then made a quick right turn. Two steps farther, there was a quick left turn.

Before we could explore further, voices reached us. I pushed Jodie behind me and snuffed out our torch. Unleathering my Colt, I stood so I could see the approaching glow of a torch on the back wall of the alcove.

We didn't have long to wait. Within minutes, the glow lit the back wall, and the muffled sound of voices reached our ears. I tightened my grip on the .44 as the torchlight grew brighter. The Kiowa were looking into the alcove. I held my breath, hoping they would give the recess nothing more than a cursory glance.

Time dragged as they studied the recess for what seemed hours, but in reality only seconds elapsed, and they moved on. I heard Jodie sigh and felt her grip relax, but we stood as we were for several more minutes. We didn't know if the Kiowa had continued down the passage or if they had turned back.

After about fifteen minutes, I whispered, "Time to go." I lit our torch. It flickered once or twice, then went out. "Hold on," I said, lighting another branch. I smiled at Jodie. She smiled bravely in return. "Let's go," I said, automatically taking her hand.

After a few steps, I noticed a difference in the floor of the cave. I lowered the torch. A dull glow reflected from the floor. Kneeling, I ran my fingers over the surface. It was smooth, almost slick. "Would you look at this?" I whispered.

Jodie knelt beside me and laid her fingers on the floor. "What caused it?"

I shook my head. "Maybe it's just a natural thing." But suddenly I had the feeling that we had stumbled back in time.

The passage widened to eight feet, the walls smooth from floor to ceiling, which itself was about twenty feet up. I shook my head and whispered over my shoulder, "People did this."

Jodie squeezed my hand in assent.

If this passage had been constructed by humans, it must lead somewhere — perhaps, with any luck, to the outside, I thought. Around the next bend, my suspicions were confirmed.

"Look," I said, pointing to a slender pole protruding from the wall a few feet above our heads.

"It's a torch," Jodie said, craning her neck so she could look up at it. "Why is it so high?"

"I don't know." I glanced around the passage. "It could be that we've stumbled into some of those caves that Joe was telling us about at the ranch. At least we'll have some light now."

Jodie looked around at me, her face a picture of childlike enthusiasm. "That's a wonderful idea." Then the delight faded from her face, replaced by a frown. "But how do we get it? Neither one of us can reach up there."

She was right. If I had been sitting on my horse, I could have reached the torch. "No, but together we can. It's simple. I'll stand under the torch, and you stand on my shoulders." I held out my hand. "Come on."

I squatted and she sat on my shoulders. I rose easily, for she was light as my ma's old goose-feather pillows. I stood facing the wall. Slowly, Jodie rose, hiking up first one knee to my shoulder, then the other.

I don't know what I expected from her, but she didn't miss a beat. She didn't whine about falling; she didn't complain about being scared. She just did what had to be done. She reached up, and after some struggling pulled the torch out and dropped it to the floor.

We lit it and, sure enough, that torch put out a light that illuminated the cave twenty feet on either side of us.

"I still don't understand why the torch was so high up," she said.

I didn't, either, but I didn't have time to worry about that peculiarity then. Later, I figured that maybe Joe's story about wagons in the caves might not be so farfetched after all. "Let's go."

We headed deeper into the cave, but as we traveled down the passageway, we noticed torches about every fifty feet.

Thirty minutes later, we stopped to rest.

Jodie studied the torch. "Where do you think it came from?"

I shrugged. "Indians, or maybe those robbers Joe told us about." I nodded to the floor of the passage. "Look how even it is." I stared at her as I gathered my thoughts. "Whoever used it, used it regularly, but I don't have any idea what for."

Chapter Six

As we rested, both of us were lost in our own thoughts. Mine were more concerned with getting us back to the ranch safely than with the origins of the place into which we had stumbled. But Jodie continued to stare at the torch.

It was time to get moving. "Let's go," I said, heading down the passage. "This hall was built for something. Let's just hope it comes out somewhere."

We lost track of time. Occasionally the passage branched off. As in the cave, I kept to the left branch, but I had the uncomfortable feeling that we were traveling in a huge circle to our right.

Once when we stopped to rest, Jodie dozed off. I decided to let her sleep a few minutes. We had heard nothing to suggest that the Kiowa had followed us into these passages.

I studied her as she slept, the way her blond hair fell across her cheek, the movement of her slender throat as she swallowed, the curl of her fingers. I leaned back against the wall and daydreamed what my ranch would be like with her on it. I shook my head slowly. "Impossible," I muttered. *But wouldn't it be nice?* I asked myself.

After an hour or so, I awakened her, and we continued our journey. "One thing I had looked forward to," she said, "was a feather mattress in Fort Worth."

"You ever been to Fort Worth?" I asked.

"No, but my father has. He's told me all about it."

The one question I asked got her to talking. She told me her father had put her in a boarding school and then a women's college up north after her mother died, and how he bought her everything she asked for and a lot she didn't. But he had taken her out of college because he had lost all his money. "Soon," she said, her voice smug with that naïveté shared by those who have never faced any of life's tests, "soon we'll have money again, and things will be the way they once were."

I didn't want to throw cold water on her plans, but I had discovered the hard way that things are never the way they used to be. Each time I returned from my wanderings, my folks and the ranch had changed. And I seemed like a stranger — not to them, but to their way of life. Then, after I returned, I slowly began to fit into the ranch again, adjusting a little every day until I belonged. *Life goes on,* I thought. *It never stays the same.*

A few minutes later, the corridor opened into a great chamber, one so large that the light from the torch barely brushed the ceiling. We paused. A thick, musty odor filled the room.

Jodie pressed up against my arm. "What is this place?"

"Who knows." The floor was still smooth. I led the way into the darkness.

We eased our way across the floor for about five minutes, and with each step, our pace slowed. *Where are we?* I wondered.

Sweat rolled down my forehead and down my back, soaking my shirt. The perimeter of light from the torch edged across the smooth floor step by step.

Suddenly, the floor disappeared, and the glow from the torch fell away into utter darkness. I jerked to a halt. "Look," I whispered, extending the torch even though we were still twenty feet from the darkness where the floor once had been.

Jodie clung to my arm. I tried to swallow, but my mouth was too dry and tasted like copper.

One step at a time, we edged toward the darkness. Drawing closer, we saw that the entire floor stopped at the edge of what appeared to be a great chasm. It seemed to bisect the chamber, or at least as far as we could see.

We eased closer. The light spilled over the edge and tumbled into the depths until the darkness finally absorbed it. I pulled a sage branch from my hip pocket and tossed it into the chasm.

Neither of us spoke as we strained to hear the sage hit bottom. Jodie slipped her hand into mine and squeezed hard, as if trying to draw strength from me. There was no sound.

I held the torch higher. The yellow flames cast their light across the pit, which appeared to be about twenty feet wide. But how long? And more important, was there a way across?

Slowly, we moved along the edge of the chasm. Five minutes later, we reached a wall, then we backtracked. This time I counted my steps. Nine hundred and thirty steps later, we discovered a rope bridge over the pit.

The bridge was unlike other rope bridges constructed in the West, but I had seen a picture of one like it in one of my mother's books. It consisted of a single rope about six inches in diameter that was meant to be walked on. The handrails were two ropes, one on either side, about four feet high and fastened to the larger one by a series of crisscrossed strands, which reminded me of the Jacob's ladder I made out of string when I was a kid.

The bridge stretched tightly between two ledges, one on each side of the pit and rising several feet above the floor. Steps had been cut into the stone leading to the ledges.

"That thing is probably so rotten with age that it'll fall to dust at the slightest touch," I said.

But it wasn't.

I climbed the stairs and inspected the bridge's rigging. Both the hand and foot ropes were knotted around thick, petrified-rock snubbing posts that in turn were attached to the floor of the chamber, where similar posts had been fitted into the ground at an acute angle.

With the point of my knife, I probed at the ropes. I didn't recognize the material from which they were made, but it wasn't horsehair or hemp. The weave was tight and the strands unbroken. There was no sag at all in the bridge. I pulled and yanked, but the ropes were taut and resilient.

I climbed back down and looked at Jodie. "I think it'll hold." We both looked up at the bridge, keeping our eyes diverted from the consuming blackness below.

She didn't reply for several moments. Finally, her eyes still on the rope bridge, she said, "I'm scared."

I laid my hand on hers. "Me, too."

"What do you think? Maybe we should go back." She looked at me as she spoke.

"No. The Kiowa are unpredictable. They know we're in here. They might camp outside for a month, just waiting for us. Or they might already be gone. You can't tell. I think the best thing is for us to chance the bridge."

Jodie swallowed hard and nodded.

"I'll go first," I said.

"What about the torch?"

I pounded the heel of my hand against my forehead. I had forgotten about the torch. There was no question — we needed it on the other side. I had no choice. "I'll take it with me."

"But how? You'll need both hands to hold on to the ropes."

"I'll just have to make it with one."

Jodie said nothing as I took the torch and climbed up the stairs. She followed right behind me.

Sometimes odd thoughts jump into my mind at the most unexpected times. As I mounted the stairs, I found myself wishing I were back on the ranch looking after the cattle. Those miserable critters looked mighty good to me at that moment.

I reached the ledge and stepped up on the rope. My boot heel slipped. I handed the torch to Jodie, sat down, and removed my boots and socks. Then I heaved them to the other side. "Now, let's see," I muttered, stepping onto the rope.

My feet, damp from my socks and boots, clung to the rope like a fly on a windowpane. "That's it," I said. "Take your boots off."

She removed them, and I tossed hers across too. Then I mounted the rope, and with the torch in front of me, started across. It was only twenty feet, but it looked like a mile. The moisture on my bare feet and the fact that the bridge was so taut helped me. Once or twice, I had to pause to regain my balance, but within seconds I reached the far side.

"Come on," I whispered to Jodie. "You can do it."

She came slowly, having to stretch to reach the hand ropes on either side. She'd take a step and then slide her hand a few inches farther along the rope.

Halfway over, she looked up at me and smiled.

"Keep your eyes —"

Suddenly, her foot slipped and she lost her balance, spilling forward off the rope. She screamed and grabbed one of the support ropes. "Matt!"

"Hold on!" I yelled, dropping the torch. "I'm coming."

"My hand's slipping. I can't hold on."

"You've got to. You hear me? You've got to!"

Upright, I took three or four steps toward her. Before I could lose my balance, I dropped to my knees, straddling the rope, and fell forward on my stomach, hoping the web on which I lay would hold.

"Hurry, Matt! Hurry!"

I scooted forward. One of her hands slipped. She screamed. She was now hanging by only one hand. She tried to grab the rope, but her body had twisted around until her back was to the bridge. She clutched blindly behind her, her slender fingers grasping frantically at the air.

I saw that she was losing her grip on the rope. Slowly the weight of her body pulled her fist open until she was hanging by only her fingers, the tips of which slowly whitened as the rope dug into her flesh.

I lunged forward and grabbed her wrist just as her fingers tore loose. She swung under me like a pendulum. "Hold on," I said between clenched teeth.

I wrapped my free arm around the rope and strained to heave her up. Although she barely tipped a hundred pounds, she was a dead weight. I paused to gather my strength.

She screamed.

Her scream pumped adrenaline into my

veins. With one heave, I pulled her up to the rope and held on until she threw a leg over. Locking my feet over the ropes behind me, I scooted back a few inches, my fingers still wrapped around her wrist. She followed. Her face was pale with fright and tears welled in her eyes, but she kept her lips pressed tightly together and her jaw set.

We both lay spread-eagle over the ropes, Jodie easing forward as I slid back. When we finally reached the ledge, we collapsed on the ground, breathing hard. After a moment, we retrieved our boots and headed on down the passage, wondering if we would ever find our way out. Then we ran into the same kind of entrance that had led us into the passage, a series of abrupt right and left turns that opened into a cave. In the distance, sunlight spilled through its mouth.

"Look!" Jodie shouted. "We made it!" She started to rush to the opening, but I grabbed her arm.

"Hold on. Let's see what's out there first."

I extinguished the torch and placed it just inside the entrance to the passage. Then we made our way to the sunlight.

Pausing just inside the narrow entrance, I slipped the rawhide loop off the hammer of the Colt as I peered through a dense growth of underbrush to study the lay of land around the cave opening. I didn't hear anything or anyone, so I pushed through the brush and into a gully filled with sandstone boulders. We had come out behind the bluffs, looking north across the prairie.

I looked back. Even as close as I was, I couldn't make out the entrance to the cave. I spoke softly. "Come on out. Everything's okay."

Jodie looked up at the sun in midsky. "The sun feels wonderful."

I grinned. "Yeah."

Suddenly, a voice froze us in our tracks. "Don't move a muscle." The words were followed by the click of a gun hammer.

Chapter Seven

Jodie and I turned as one. Standing above us on a red crown of sandstone was Billy Wayne, the young man who rode with Rafe Cutler. He held a Winchester, aimed directly at us. The crooked grin on his face disappeared when he saw Jodie. "Why — you're a woman," he gasped.

I've got to hand it to Jodie. She faced him and the Winchester as coolly as anyone, just as calmly as she'd handled the entire ordeal in the cave. "Well, I guess that makes you a brave man, doesn't it?" she said, her voice filled with sarcasm. "Only a brave man holds a gun on a woman."

It appeared she had changed, and for the better.

He winced as her words slapped his face, which had yet to see much of a beard. "I — I —" He swallowed hard, then set his jaw. "Just don't worry about that," he said gruffly.

He looked at me. "You. Put those hands up." He gestured with the muzzle of the Winchester. "Step back."

As I obeyed his orders, I dragged my hand over the butt of my revolver, hooking my thumb into the rawhide loop and flipping it off the hammer. I knew that somehow, some way, I had to take him. We couldn't afford to fall into Cutler's hands.

He glanced at his feet. I grinned inwardly when I recognized his predicament. The sandstone boulder on which he stood was shaped like an egg, and he was standing on the small end. Its sides were smooth. The only way he could have scaled it was on his hands and knees.

Deliberately, I kept my eyes on his face. Our chances were much better if he didn't know I was aware of his dilemma. Keeping my hands high over my head, I tensed my muscles, getting ready for just the right moment.

I was not a fast gun, and having to bring my hand from over my head would take extra time, maybe too much time. But I didn't see what choice I had.

He sat down on the side of the ledge and scooted forward, all the while keeping the muzzle of the Winchester trained on me. He planned to scoot down the boulder just as if it were a slide.

I steadied myself.

He pushed forward and started his slide.

Out of the corner of my eye, I saw Jodie drop to the ground. Billy jerked the muzzle toward her, and I dropped my hand and leaped to my right. I hit the ground rolling and firing.

A slug tore up a chunk of sand by my head. I rolled again and fired. This time, I found Billy in my sights as his feet hit the ground. My slug caught him in the chest and spun him around. He slammed into the boulder, then bounced to the ground.

I lay still, my revolver trained on the inert young man. Cautiously, I rose and approached him. I heard Jodie behind me, but I kept my eyes on Billy.

She touched my arm as I looked down on the young man. "Get his gun," I said.

Moving quickly, she picked up the Winchester and took his revolver. I holstered my own revolver and turned him over. Relief washed over me when I saw that he was still breathing, but the stain on his shirt was spreading.

"Is he dead?" Jodie whispered.

I shook my head. "Not yet, but he will be if we don't stop the bleeding." I removed and folded his bandanna, then laid it over the wound. "Press down on this to stop the blood."

Without a word, Jodie did as I said while I tore a strip from the bottom of my shirt to wrap around his chest.

"What now?" Jodie asked as I snugged the

bandage down tight on his wound. "He needs more doctoring than we can give him."

"I know." I rose and looked around. "He's bound to have hitched his horse around here somewhere. We'll throw him over the saddle, and you can ride behind." I nodded to the north. "My place is about twenty miles that way. There's water and shelter there. You can stay with him while I ride on to the Eastlands' for a wagon."

"Then what? I hope you don't waste too much time on that outlaw. We still have to find my father."

I stared at her. Right before my eyes, she had changed back into that selfish brat again. I had started to thank her for distracting Billy, but the thanks died in my throat. And then I remembered my foolish dream about her being on my ranch with me. *Not in my lifetime,* I told myself. All I wanted to do was to get her back to the ranch and be rid of her.

I went searching for Billy's horse. After clambering over some rocks, I had poised to leap to another ledge a few feet away when a movement on the ledge stopped me. I looked closer and a chill ran up my spine. A rattlesnake lay sunning at my feet, its mottled scales a sharp contrast to the red sandstone. I backed away and skirted the snake, noting as I did a large, dark hole beneath the overhang.

I headed down the arroyo and found the horse standing patiently around the first bend. Fortunately, Billy carried a canteen. I shook it. Half full. That would have to do.

I eased the wounded young outlaw into his saddle and lashed him down. He slumped forward over the saddle horn. "Your turn," I said, holding the stirrup for Jodie. After she mounted, I took the reins and struck out for my spread. "You'll have to hold him," I said over my shoulder.

"How long before we reach your ranch?"

"Long enough."

"Just how long is 'long enough'?" Her voice was testy.

"Midnight or thereabouts."

I heard her groan, and I grinned at the thought of her discomfort. But my grin quickly faded as I remembered what lay ahead of us. Twenty miles of prairie with Kiowa during the day and rattlesnakes at night. I pulled my hat down over my eyes and glanced at my feet. Boots weren't made for walking, but right then I was glad I had them on. Come night, the tough leather would offer some protection against a snakebite.

The afternoon dragged. The heat rose in waves, contorting the horizon. I tried to keep us in the low spots, arroyos, gullies, and along the base of small rises — any place that would cut our silhouette. My feet sank in the hot sand, and every step was like pulling my foot out of thick mud.

After four hours of silence, Jodie spoke. "I'm thirsty."

I hated to stop. I had reached the point where it was easier to put one foot in front of the other than come to a halt.

"Did you hear me?"

I jerked to a halt and looked up at her. Her face was flushed, and her hair clung like string to her damp face. Her shirt was soaked. From the way she glared at me, I could see Ben Ross in her. Maybe that was why she was so spoiled. After her mother died, her father gave her everything. Then why had she been so different back in the cave? *Who knows,* I told myself, *and who cares?*

"Well, are you going to give me the canteen?"

Without a word, I removed the canteen from the saddle horn. Jodie reached for it with a satisfied look on her face.

"Not yet," I said, pouring some in my cupped hand and holding it for the horse.

"What are you doing that for?"

I was growing mighty tired of her. "If you don't know, then I can't explain it to you."

After watering the horse, I tipped Billy's head sideways and poured some water over his lips. It just ran onto the ground. Then I handed the canteen to Jodie. "Only a couple of swallows. We've got a long way to go."

She stared at me defiantly and turned up the canteen. She took half a dozen deep swallows before I could jerk it away from her. "I told you not to guzzle it!" I said angrily. "We need to ration it in case we don't make it to my place tonight."

She tossed her head. "I don't care. I was thirsty."

Shaking my head, I turned away from her and took a sip of water and sloshed it around in my mouth. One more sip, and I stuck the cork back in the canteen. It would be dark in a few hours. The cool night would slake our thirst.

Suddenly, I drew up. Dark silhouettes appeared on the horizon. They were too distant to discern who they were, but there were six of them, and they traveled single file. Indians. No doubt about it. Quickly, I led the horse to a nearby arroyo.

"Stay here," I said to Jodie as I slipped out the saddle gun and shucked a cartridge into the chamber. Billy moaned.

I clambered up the side of the arroyo and peered over the top of the sage. My heart pounded against my chest. They had turned directly toward us.

Taking a deep breath, I forced myself to think calmly. They gave no indication of having spotted us. Had they seen us, they would be charging at a full gallop instead of loafing along in a lazy stroll. But still, if they continued in our direction, they would stumble right into our laps.

I hurried back into the arroyo. The sandy bed showed much travel since the last rain, enough that our sign blended right in. "They're coming our way," I whispered. Grabbing the reins, I led the horse down the arroyo at a trot. With luck, we could skirt the Indians.

Ten minutes later, I stopped. Gasping for breath, I leaned forward, my hands on my knees, my chest heaving. Sharp pains shot through my arches and knifed up my legs.

"What's wrong?"

I pointed ahead of us, too winded to speak.

"What is it?"

When I got my breath back, I explained, "This arroyo is shallowing out. Any farther, and they'll spot us."

"So what do we do? Just wait here?"

"That's what we do. Just wait."

I slipped to the top of the arroyo and searched the prairie for the Indians. They had dropped out of sight. I mulled over their disappearance for a moment, until I realized where they were — in this same arroyo. We had to move, and move fast.

I reached for my revolver, planning to use the butt as a hammer to knock the heels off my boots. I knew from having witnessed a cowboy hobbling into our ranch one day that another few miles of running or walking in those heels would cripple my arches.

A wild cry made me look up. Three Kiowa had just swept around a bend in the arroyo and were charging down on us at a full gallop. Two were headed toward me, and the third charged Jodie and the wounded outlaw.

Cursing myself for not bringing the saddle gun with me, I took careful aim with the Colt and squeezed off a shot when the first Kiowa was less than twenty yards from me. The impact of the one-hundred-and-eighty-grain slug knocked him out of his saddle.

The second Kiowa stood in his stirrups, sighting down the barrel of an old Springfield trapdoor with a muzzle that looked like a .50 or one of those older modified .58s. Before I could turn my .44 on him, he swept past, but the Springfield misfired. I fired. The slug caught him in the middle of the back and sent him sprawling across the neck of his pony.

In the meantime, Jodie had leaped to the ground and was screaming and kicking at the Indian who was trying to grab the reins of her horse. I threw a shot in his direction. He cried out and grabbed his shoulder. Without a second's hesitation, he drove his heels into his pony's flanks and raced back down the arroyo.

"Are you all right?" I called out to Jodie as I ran back to her.

Her face was white, but her jaw had a set to it that I had to admire. "I think so."

I rounded up the two Indian ponies, and we swung onto them. "Let's get out of here!" I yelled, grabbing the reins of Billy's horse and heeling my pony. We cut across the prairie for my ranch.

I kept looking over my shoulder, expecting to see the other Kiowa at any time. The unconscious outlaw slowed us. I had him lashed down good and snug, but we still lost time.

Finally I saw what I had been dreading. Dark figures appeared on the horizon behind us. Pulling up next to Jodie, I gave her the reins to the outlaw's mount. "Keep going. I'm falling back." Before I did, I retrieved Billy's saddle gun. At least I could keep the Kiowa at a distance.

She nodded and drove her heels into the laboring pony's flanks. I slowed. We covered another two or three miles before the Kiowa closed to within a hundred yards of me. I looked for Jodie. She was a half a mile ahead.

I gave the pony his head. I didn't want Jodie too far away in case she ran into trouble.

When I had drawn within a quarter of a mile of her, I reined up the pony and threw a couple of slugs at the pursuing Indians. The Kiowa flared to one side and slowed. One pulled a carbine and aimed at me. He lowered it, fumbled with it, then shouldered it again. Still nothing.

While he fumbled with his saddle gun the next time, I held just over his head and squeezed off a round. His horse spun and reared, almost unseating the Kiowa, who dropped his rifle and clung to his pony's mane.

I turned back after Jodie.

The Kiowa milled about a few minutes, then rode after me. Half a mile farther, I stopped and fired at them again, and again they fell back, milled around, shook their fists at me, then followed again.

The leapfrog game continued until dark. I pointed out the North Star to Jodie. "Head directly for that star. I'll catch up with you."

She nodded. I could tell she was frightened, but she never once complained.

I fell back and hid in a shallow gully, hoping that the Kiowa would continue in a straight course. If they swung wide and I missed them, Jodie could be in big trouble. The darkness surrounding me was complete except for the

96

sage silhouetted against the stars.

Minutes later, the sound of hooves cut through the night. I grinned. The Kiowa were coming straight toward me. I cocked the saddle gun, and as soon as the first shadow appeared against the starlit night, I fired. I continued to fire as fast as I could, shucking one cartridge after another into the chamber.

I don't know if I hit them or not, but when the echoes died away, I heard hoofbeats heading south.

Sighing with relief, I caught up with Jodie, and by midnight we had reached my ranch. I left them there, and hurriedly rode on to the Eastland ranch. I was anxious to get Jodie off my hands, for deliberately or otherwise she had caused me more problems than a one-armed cowpoke trying to hog-tie a squawking calf.

During the ride back to the Eastland ranch, I tried to look at our predicament from every angle, but none of them made much sense. At the ranch, I hurriedly swapped the pony for a big roan gelding about sixteen hands high and deep-chested for stamina. I headed back to my spread, followed by Joe and Martha in the buggy.

Topping a sand hill overlooking my ranch, I pulled up and stared down at the partially demolished soddy. Nothing moved, but then I didn't expect to see anything. I had told Jodie to remain inside and keep the wounded outlaw quiet.

Joe stopped the wagon beside me.

"Where is she?" Martha asked. "It sure is quiet down there."

The prairie wind moaned as it brushed through the sage, adding to the sense of foreboding that had suddenly sent a chill down my spine. Something was wrong. "They're in there," I replied, more in an effort to convince myself than Martha. "I told her not to stick her head outside."

Flipping the rawhide loop off the hammer of my .44, I urged the roan down the hill, hoping at every step that Jodie would come rushing from the soddy, her blond hair flying and white teeth glistening in a broad smile.

But she didn't. After a search of the ranch, we still couldn't find her. She had disappeared along with the wounded outlaw.

Joe and I studied the hard-packed earth around the soddy. All we could find were the scars made by horseshoes. We spread our search beyond the yard, and there we stumbled across sign. There were six, maybe seven riders, best I could figure. One set of tracks cut deeper. Jodie and the outlaw were probably on that horse, for it brought up the tail end. That meant they were being led.

"Headed west," Joe said.

I studied the western horizon, an undulating line that quivered in the rising waves of heat.

"Kiowa, you figure?" he asked, resting the breech of his Winchester on his shoulder, his finger still on the trigger and the rifle still cocked.

"Could be, though they're heading west toward Comanche country. Palo Duro Canyon is out there."

"I wonder what's going on? Quanah Parker's given up to the military, leastwise that's what they've been saying back in Antelope Flats."

I holstered my .44. "I heard that too. But even if that great war chief did give up, there are bound to be some renegades who chose to go out on their own, young braves who never had the chance to prove their manhood."

Joe pulled the Winchester down and lowered the hammer to safety. "Fool way to prove they're men."

"Could be that's the only way they know, Joe," I said, remembering some of my conversations with Many Dogs while he was healing up on our place.

He grunted and turned back to the buggy

as I swung into the saddle. "Joe, you and Martha head on back to the ranch. I'll stop off at the tank and fill my canteen, then I'll go after them."

With a terse nod, he slapped the reins against his horse's rump. "Take care."

"You too," I said as I nudged the roan into a gentle lope.

The sign was easy to read, so easy in fact that the hair on the back of my neck prickled when I wondered if someone had deliberately wanted me to follow it. Who? Kiowa? Cutler's bunch? They knew someone was meddling in their business. One of their own had been killed, another was missing. That was enough to rub anyone the wrong way.

But whoever it was, Cutler or Indians, I decided not let them see me first.

The trail bore due west, across the rolling prairie that stretched endlessly from horizon to horizon. From past travels, I knew that Palo Duro Canyon was a hard journey of a couple of days, but it could be done.

From time to time, the sandy prairie rolled over a stretch of clay that gave me a better handle on who I was following. Not much better, I decided when I saw that all the horses were shod.

But the more I studied the sign, the more I thought that I was following a band of Indians. While most Indians, especially the Kiowa, paid close attention to their mounts, they discounted the value of horseshoes. And as a result of that ignorance and the lack of shoeing facilities, they often failed to keep their animals' shoes in good shape.

The shoes on two of the horses were in poor condition, certain to bring on lameness within a few weeks. But, I reminded myself with the other side of the argument, Cutler's bunch could have been on the run so long that they hadn't spared the time to get their own animals shod.

Whoever it was, they weren't slowing their pace. They were obviously bent on reaching Palo Duro by the next day.

I sipped at the canteen throughout the afternoon. My stomach growled, and I tried to remember how long it had been since I had eaten. Ahead of me, a prairie grouse burst from cover. I reached for my saddle gun, then paused.

A gunshot would echo for miles across the silent prairie. I didn't want to give my quarry any more aid than I could help. No, tonight I would have to settle for water and whatever I could dig up — which was an unlucky rattlesnake that I quickly cooked before sundown. While the meat broiled, I kept watch on the prairie around me. My quarry could be miles away, or they could be in the next arroyo.

After the meal, I got back on the trail until dark. When I could no longer see the trail, I rode north fifteen minutes and bedded down in a shallow arroyo, careful to leave the saddle on my roan.

The next morning, as soon as it was light enough to read sign, I was on their trail. Soon I would know if I was following Cutler or Indians. They must have stopped for the night, and no one can mistake the white man's camp for an Indian's.

Two hours later, I found where they had camped. I had been right. The camp told me who I followed — Indians. But, strangely enough, no effort had been made to erase evidence of their camp.

The fire had been small and impressions of bodies surrounded the coals, for Indians slept in a circle around the fire with the prisoners inside. The stakes they had used to spread-eagle their prisoners lay scattered about. That was a practice of the Comanche, so the band harbored at least one or two of that tribe. Drops of blood stained the sand. Billy was still hanging on. He appeared to be a tough kid. I hoped he was.

The sandy soil began to give way to a thicker loam. We were nearing Palo Duro and the showdown.

In midafternoon, I topped out on the rim overlooking the vast and forbidding canyon. Quickly dismounting, I tied the roan to a small shrub so he could graze on the sparse grass while I lay on my stomach and peered down into the canyon.

Rocky and craggy on the rims, the canyon was filled with wiry underbrush and thick grass. As I stared down into the ominously silent crags and gullies, I knew I couldn't follow the Indian party into the canyon during daylight. I would have to go after dark, so all I could do now was wait and watch, and hope that I could spot their fire after dark.

Down below, the only movement was the wind rocking the cedar and wild laurels. Above the canyon, a lone eagle circled, searching for its own quarry.

Chapter Eight

No sooner had the sun set and darkness spilled into the canyon than I spotted their campfire. Although the fire was small, it was very visible. The back of my neck prickled again. They were making no effort to hide the fire. It was as if they were trying to pull me in, or defy me to find them.

Whichever it was, I was going in. Leading the roan, I dropped down into the canyon and hobbled him in a hollow filled with spindly shrubs and sparse grass. It was poor graze, but it would have to do. From where I stood, about halfway down the canyon wall, I could see the fire blazing in one of the southwestern fingers of the canyon.

Palming my .44, I dropped down into the canyon, taking care to stay in the shadows while at the same time not touching the underbrush for fear of making slight scraping sounds.

As I grew closer, a faint chanting reached my ears. I couldn't see the fire because of the thick undergrowth, but the glow shone above the small shrubs. After I reached the canyon floor, I moved so slowly that I covered no more than three hundred feet in an hour. Each time I reached a new hiding place, I paused to study every shadow around me.

Finally, I slipped behind a boulder on a small rise overlooking the campfire. Peering around the base of the boulder, I saw my quarry for the first time. A sudden premonition tightened my muscles. There were only three Indians in camp, all Kiowa. They knelt at the fire, their backs to me, chanting.

I strained my ears. Three Indians were missing. Did that mean they had been waiting for me? But I had moved slowly and carefully.

To one side of the fire, Jodie knelt beside the young outlaw. Even in the orange glow of the campfire, I could see the pale sign of death in his face. I glanced over my shoulder. I had no idea where the other braves were, but if I planned on doing something, now was the time.

Moving silently, I rose to my feet and like a spider over webs approached the camp in a crouch, my eyes locked on the three braves, my finger tight against the trigger.

Jodie looked up. Her lips parted, but I silenced her with my hand. Suddenly, her eyes flicked past me and her mouth widened in a scream.

Before I could react, a powerful force struck me on the back of my head, sending me tumbling head over heels into a deep, dark well.

I awoke with a throbbing skull and bound wrists.

The first voice I heard was Jodie's. "Oh, Matt, you're awake — you're alive."

"It . . . it looks that way," I mumbled, my head pounding so fiercely that my ears hurt. "Wh-what happened?"

"They were waiting for you. If only I had seen you. . . . One was on that boulder above you."

I groaned with frustration. I had walked into their hands just like a greener. Clenching my teeth against the throbbing headache, I looked around. We were in a tepee. "Where are we?"

"They moved us up the canyon. That camp last night was just a trap."

Before I could reply, the buffalo flap swung open and a swarthy brave with a scarred face stepped in. His eyes glared at me malevolently. "You live. Good."

He stared down at me, his black eyes filled with hate. A diagonal scar ran from his hairline across the bridge of his nose to his chin. The thickened tissue of the scar twisted his lips into a grotesque, permanent sneer.

I returned his look and remained silent. I wouldn't give him the satisfaction of speaking first. Whatever he wanted us to know, he would have to offer it. We wouldn't beg to know what plans they had for us.

The smile on his lips broadened as he realized I wouldn't speak. He understood the game and it amused him. Finally, he said, "You know our ways. That is good. But tomorrow, I will teach you how long it takes a man to die."

Jodie caught her breath.

I extended my bound wrists, saying, "It is easy to be brave when your enemy is helpless."

He shrugged and glanced at Jodie. "I have other preparations to make for tomorrow," he replied, turning on his heel and leaving the tepee.

"Here," I said, holding up my hands to Jodie, who quickly freed my bonds.

"What's going to happen to us?" she asked.

She was frightened, and I didn't blame her. I couldn't tell her that they would probably kill me, permit Billy to die, and then take her into their band. One of the braves would marry her — at least until he tired of her.

"I don't know," I lied. "If I had some idea what was going on, then maybe we could do something. We're in Comanche country, but the Comanche have surrendered to the Army. From what I've seen, these are Kiowa. They've been on the warpath for the last several months. But don't worry. We'll figure out something."

I didn't want to alarm her any more, but at the moment I didn't have the slightest idea what we were going to do. All I knew was that we would do something. Sitting around waiting to be the main character in one of the Kiowa's cruel games was not my idea of a way to spend a pleasant afternoon.

First, I checked Billy. I shook my head. His pulse was weak, and his breathing was shallow. He couldn't last another day. A momentary pang of regret nagged at me, but I reminded myself that my slug would not have killed him if I could have put him in the ministering hands of Martha Eastland. And, as much as I hated to think it, if he died, we would not be saddled with a wounded man when we attempted to escape.

Motioning for Jodie to remain silent, I crouched by the buffalo flap that covered the front opening and parted the flap just enough to study the camp. There were over two dozen tepees set up, and the low murmur of a busy camp filled the air. The one thing missing that I had hoped to see was an Indian squaw, but there were none. Then who had set up the tepees? Or were the structures left behind by Quanah Parker's Comanche?

There was no question at all about the intent of the preparations outside. This was a war camp, and fired-up braves on the warpath were not going to take prisoners with them.

"What do you see?" Jodie scooted closer to me.

"Not much. This is just a temporary camp. When they finish with their fun tomorrow, they'll head out to hit more ranches."

She swallowed hard. I forced a smile and laid my hand on hers. "Don't worry. I'll think of something to get us out of this mess."

She gazed up at me, her chin quivering. Suddenly, she ducked her head and pressed her hands against her face. Soft sobs shook her shoulders. "If only I hadn't run away from the ranch. None of this would have happened."

Awkwardly, I put my arm around her shoulders and tried to comfort her. "Nobody's to blame. What's happened has happened. What we've got to do now is figure out how to get out of here."

After a few more minutes, her sobs subsided and she looked up into my face with teary eyes. "Can you get us out of here?"

"I'll do my best. I've got an idea." I didn't, but a small lie wouldn't make our predicament any worse.

She forced a weak smile, and I turned back to the opening in the buffalo flap.

The heat in the closed tepee was suffocating.

And as the afternoon lengthened, the heat increased. We did our best to make Billy comfortable, but with no medicine or water, we were helpless. Slowly he slipped deeper and deeper into the arms of death.

In midafternoon at the crest of the rising temperature, a Kiowa brave threw open the flap and rolled up the base of the tepee to permit a cooling breeze. Camp sounds were thus sharpened, an advantage for us since we were better able to discern the Indians' actions. Just before dusk, the thud of approaching hoofbeats silenced the low voices in the camp.

I laid my cheek to the ground and peered through the space at the bottom of the tepee, but I could see nothing. Raised voices and shouts echoed all around.

"Who is it? Can you see anything?" Jodie was pressed up against me.

"Not a thing."

But from the rising voices and the intensity of the words, it was obvious that there was a strong disagreement taking place. Hope leaped in my heart. This could be our chance. I glanced at Billy. His mouth was open and he was gasping for breath.

We couldn't leave him. But this might be our only opportunity to flee. I heard the arguing braves moving in our direction. I looked into Jodie's eyes. She read my thoughts. A grim smile played over her lips, and I knelt by the dying man and laid my hand on his sweaty forehead.

Then Many Dogs stepped into the tepee and said, "My brother."

I jumped to my feet and stared at him, momentarily confused. Was he part of this renegade band? Had he stooped so low as to kidnap a young woman?

His dark eyes studied my face, and I could tell from his expression that he had read my thoughts. He extended his arm, and my ears burned in shame. I knew this man, and there was no way on earth that he would turn renegade or kidnap a woman.

I took his arm, our hands grasping each other's forearm. "Brother," I replied.

He glanced at Jodie, who hovered behind me. "She is well?"

"Yes. Just frightened, but she is well." I turned to Jodie. "This is Many Dogs. He is the one who saw us in the cave on the river."

She smiled. "Thank you for not giving us away."

He grunted. "And that one," he said, nodding to the young boy at our feet.

"Dying."

Without a word, Many Dogs knelt, his braids dangling in front of him. He threw them back over his shoulders as he inspected the wound and laid his hand on the boy's forehead. He rose and left the tepee, returning moments later with two bowls of fresh water, one for us and one for Billy.

With gentle hands, Many Dogs cleansed the wound, which started to bleed again. Then he opened the parfleche pouch that he carried around his waist and sprinkled powder on the wound. The bleeding ceased instantly. "He is hot. This will help," he said, pouring a pinch of the powder into the bowl of water, and then tilting Billy's head so he could drink.

When Billy finished, Many Dogs turned to face us. "Sit." He crossed his legs and gave us a wry smile. "You have made some problems for yourself, my brother."

I glanced out the open flap and shook my head. "We weren't bothering them," I said angrily. "They came into my home and took her and the wounded boy while I was gone."

Many Dogs frowned at the accusation in my voice. "They are men who do not follow our leaders, just as you have men who do not obey your own laws. But it was the white man who paid Badger That Kills to steal the woman."

I stared at Many Dogs in surprise. "What did you say?"

He grunted. "That is true. Two white men gave Badger That Kills two pieces of gold coin to take the woman and keep her away from the ranch for ten sleeps. That is all I know."

I looked at Jodie, who stared at Many Dogs in shock. "Cutler," I muttered.

"I do not know the name."

"I do," I said. "I know it well." I paused, then asked, "Can you get us out of here?"

He shrugged his broad shoulders. "Badger That Kills is the leader here. He and many of our people have made peace with those of Parker's Comanche who refused to surrender." He shook his head slowly. "They do not hear the wisdom of peace."

At that moment, loud voices approached the tepee. The brave with the disfigured face stepped inside. He glared at me, then at Many Dogs. "I will kill the white man in the Test of the Cleansing with the rising of the sun tomorrow," he said.

Many Dogs rose majestically and faced the brave. "Badger That Kills forgets that the test must be sanctified by our holy man. Or do the followers of Lone Wolf and Sky Walker need no holy man?"

Badger That Kills glared at Many Dogs, then turned his blazing eyes on me, eyes filled with so much venom that they ate away a man's soul like a malignant growth. "That will be time enough," he said with a mocking laugh.

"And," Many Dogs interrupted, "until that time, they are my guests and they will be treated as such."

Badger That Kills opened his mouth, then clamped it shut. A cunning gleam lit his eyes, then he stormed away, followed by his men.

Many Dogs turned back to us and smiled. "You are safe for two days. Then the holy man comes."

"What happens then?" Jodie asked.

"Then my brother will be forced to fight Badger That Kills."

A cold chill enveloped me. "What kind of fight?"

Many Dogs' eyes softened when he looked at me. "It is the Test of the Cleansing."

"What kind of weapons?"

"Knives."

"Is he good?"

"Yes. See his face. Hear his name. Badger That Kills has fought this test more than twenty times."

"So, that means. . . ." I paused and took a deep breath to still the pounding in my chest.

Many Dogs nodded. "He has killed twenty men."

Jodie gasped, and I closed my eyes against the sudden bitterness that rose in my throat.

★ ★ ★

After a meal of charred horsemeat and a handful of ground corn, we sat and talked in the tepee until the late hours. The flickering flames from the campfire threw shadows through the front opening, illuminating our faces with an eerie orange glow. An unspoken tension filled the tepee.

Many Dogs explained all that had happened among the Indians. This band of Comanche and Kiowa, led by Badger That Kills, followed the general leadership of Sky Walker, an Indian for whom the Army had been searching over a year. The Kiowa chieftain, Kicking Bird, was on the reservation at Fort Sill, pleading with his people to come in and stop fighting.

During a pause in our conversation, we noted that Billy's breathing had become deeper and more regular. Soon, Jodie slept. Only Many Dogs and I remained awake. The tension remained. Each of us recognized it.

Outside, an owl hooted.

Finally, I broke the tension, saying what neither of us wanted to say. "Can I slay Badger That Kills?"

Many Dogs stared at me for a long minute, his brows knitted in pain. "We have two days. I will show you all I know." The answer was not direct, but what he didn't say answered my question. "Who knows? Perhaps the Sun and the Moon will decide there will be no test."

I grinned. "I do not have that luck, my brother."

He shrugged. "Nor do I."

Despite the impending fight to the death, I slept well that night. The next day, and the one following, Many Dogs taught me as much as I could absorb concerning the test. Mentally, there was no problem, but acquiring the physical skills was next to impossible.

The Test of the Cleansing allowed a Kiowa brave to free his soul of the evil he had committed by the slaying of an enemy. The two combatants were joined at the wrist by a six-foot length of rope. Strict rules were observed in the fight: The only weapon used was a knife, no fists or wrestling holds were allowed, just knives and the rope. The bound arm could not be touched by a blade.

During those two days, the quality of our meals improved dramatically. When I mentioned it to Many Dogs, he grinned and whispered, "I shamed Badger That Kills by asking if he planned to kill a man weakened by hunger." His grin broadened. "After all," he added, "how much glory is there in stepping on a helpless bug?"

I feigned hurt. "You compare me to a bug?"

His conviviality faded into a grim smile. "I compare you to anything, my brother, to keep you from Badger That Kills."

His words sobered me. I looked into his eyes. "Thank you" was all I could say.

And then we returned to work, fastening a strip of rawhide about our wrists and practicing the basic moves, parrying and thrusting. "You are faster than Badger That Kills, and I believe you to have more strength," Many Dogs said. "You must use these strengths to offset his skill. You will be injured, do not doubt that. But if the gods smile, perhaps Badger That Kills will make a mistake."

I nodded and grimly continued to practice. Staking my life on another's mistake was not reassuring.

Time and again during our practice, Many Dogs would slip one of my thrusts and bring the blade of his knife against my chest. He worked with me patiently, schooling me as quickly as humanly possible.

Jodie sat nearby and watched, her eyes wide with apprehension. I know what was flashing through her mind. What would happen to her if I lost?

On the last night, I couldn't sleep. Myriad thoughts filled my mind. Although I never wished to see anything in creation harmed without just cause, I couldn't help wishing that the holy man would somehow be detained. But as the dawn neared, I realized that soon all would be in my hands. My only hope was that despite my wounds, I would remain in the contest until I could find Badger That Kills' weakness.

Just before false dawn, I dozed. Seconds later, Many Dogs shook me awake. "It is time."

Instantly awake, I looked up at him. "The holy man?"

With a somber expression, he nodded. "He is here."

I glanced at Jodie, hoping that she still slept, that the test would be over before she awakened, but she stared at me with wide eyes. I grinned and sat up.

My heart pounded against my chest, and I tried to still the churning in my stomach. "Well, let's get this over with so we can get back to the ranch."

Many Dogs extended his hand. "Wear these." He held a pair of moccasins. He gestured to my boots.

Remembering how the sand back in the arroyo had clung to my boots like mud, I quickly shucked them and slipped into the moccasins. They were a perfect fit. I moved my toes, noticing just how sensitive my feet were to the ground beneath me.

He looked at Jodie. "You must stay."

"But —"

I shook my head. "You're better off here. They can get worked up mighty fast sometimes."

She nodded and gave me a weak smile.

Many Dogs looked at me. "He will try to jerk you off balance at first. You must dig your heels into the sand." Without waiting for a reply, he turned and left the tepee.

The entire band was gathered in a great circle on the sandy floor of an adjoining finger of the canyon, over a mile from the camp. Beyond them was a tiny stream. Badger That Kills waited in the center of the circle, his eyes gloating, his twisted lips sneering.

Many Dogs and I pushed through the circle, and I stopped in front of Badger That Kills. I was half a head taller. We stared into each other's eyes.

The holy man shuffled around the inner perimeter of the circle spreading some kind of powder and chanting in a tongue I could not understand. I kept my eyes on Badger That Kills. My hands grew damp, and I drew my tongue across my dry lips to wet them.

After the holy man's blessing, our left wrists were joined by a six-foot length of braided rawhide, and we were each given identical knives: six-inch, double-edged blades with a

119

deer-horn handle.

Then the holy man said, "The spirits watch from above. This test must be taken with honor. Death is better for a man than disgrace."

While he spoke, I shifted the knife in my palm until I had a firm, comfortable grip. I remembered Many Dogs' words, and dug my heels into the sand, trying not to be obvious. I tried to relax, but every muscle was taut, awaiting the expected jerk on the rawhide.

As soon as the holy man ceased, Badger That Kills gave a wild scream and jerked backward, hoping to yank me off balance and end the fight quickly. The rope jerked against my bent arm, but I held firm, and in the next instant I pulled on it myself, putting the weight of my whole body into the effort.

Surprised by the unexpected resistance, Badger That Kills lurched forward. I leaped to meet him, slashing at his huge chest beneath his left arm. He spun aside, but not before I drew first blood, an ugly wound between his lower ribs.

His face ran a gamut of emotions, from shock to surprise to rage. But I had had my chance. I wouldn't catch him off guard again.

Gathering the rope in his left hand, he pulled us together as we circled to the right. I balanced myself on the balls of my feet, keeping my weight evenly distributed.

He jerked on the rope and slashed. I parried, but the tip of his blade caught my left arm as he drew back.

Several murmurs of disapproval erupted from the onlooking braves. Badger That Kills held up his knife to show that it was an accident, but from the sneer on his face, I knew that the move had been deliberate.

But now I realized the value of gathering rope, to provide slack in such an instance, to keep from being yanked onto a blade. He leaped forward and made a sweeping slash that would have ripped me from hip to hip, but I jumped back easily.

Knees bent, I circled, my eyes on his. Sweat poured down my forehead. He thrust. I parried. Then we circled again. I thrust; he parried, slipped the thrust, and sidestepped, causing me to lose my balance and stumble past him.

He tripped me, and I struck the ground. Immediately I rolled over and bunched my legs just as he leaped. I lashed out with my feet, catching him in the chest and knocking him back against the rope. I leaped to my feet and dropped back into a defensive posture. For the first time, I felt a glimmer of hope. He had not expected my speed.

Anger curled his lips. He thrust and stepped

forward, thrusting again. I parried, but his blade slipped and almost sliced across my chest at the base of my throat. "Now, White Eyes, I will cut your heart out," he growled.

He faked a thrust, but I didn't fall for it. He thrust again, and this time I let the blade follow through and grabbed his wrist with my left hand, bringing my own blade in a sweeping strike from below my right hip.

He saw the blade coming and spun to his right. My blade narrowly missed him, but it came close enough to draw murmurs of approval from the onlooking Indians. No sooner had he spun to his right than he spun back to his left, slashing with his blade.

I jumped back, but not before it caught me across the abdomen. A cruel grin played over his twisted lips. His brown body glistened in the blistering sun.

By this time I knew the only way either one of us could defeat the other was by wearing him down. Badger That Kills knew it too, for whenever one of the braves laughed, his disfigured face contorted into a grimace. He had been expected to slay me easily and he had not. That was defeat enough.

Suddenly, he threw a vicious attack at me, stepping forward in giant strides, slashing his dancing blade from side to side. I stepped back, casting a quick glance over my shoulder to see what lay behind. Then I saw an opening.

I had a foot of rope gathered in my hand. I waited. He stepped forward with his left foot and slashed. I yanked on the rope, using his forward momentum to jerk him toward me. At the same time, I threw up my left arm, which deflected his backward slash above my head.

Using the loose rope I had gathered, I spun it over his head with my left hand and gave another jerk, spinning him in a full circle. I leaped forward and slashed at him, hitting one of his pectoral muscles.

My move brought shouts of approval from the braves, shouts that enraged Badger That Kills and drove him into a fury. He screamed and scooped up a handful of sand and threw it in my eyes, blinding me.

Shouts of protest and anger erupted from the crowd, but I knew that wouldn't stop the crazed Kiowa. I leaped aside and slashed out blindly before me, hoping to hold him off until I could see again.

In the next instant, a gunshot exploded nearby, and I felt a jerk at the end of the rope. Struggling to open my eyes, I saw Badger That Kills sprawled on the sand before me.

Many Dogs stepped forward, smoke drifting from the muzzle of his Winchester. "The test is for honor. Badger That Kills lies in disgrace."

The other braves nodded their agreement, one of them even slashing the rawhide from my wrist.

"Now you go home," Many Dogs said. "We take you."

During the ride back to the ranch, Many Dogs asked me about my horse.

"Socks? One of your people has him. I lost him down at the caves. You think you can find him?"

"I will try."

"While you're looking, you might see if you can find the woman's horse. A pinto."

Many Dogs nodded. "I will. But you must remember, my brother, the white man has failed to take the woman this time. He will try again."

I nodded. "Don't worry. I will watch her."

Chapter Nine

The next evening, the Eastland family looked on with amazement as Many Dogs and the band of renegades dropped us off at their ranch. Two of the braves helped Billy Wayne down from his horse and carried him into the soddy.

Martha put him in bed and hovered over him like an old mother hen. Mercy tagged after me, wanting to be sure I wasn't hurt. Jodie followed me about with her eyes, always asking the silent question, *When are you going after my father?* But not once did she voice her concern, yet every time I looked at her, I expected to hear the words pour from her lips.

Joe and I were sitting in the kitchen drinking coffee when Martha rushed in and told us that Billy had mentioned Ben's name. That's what we had been waiting for. Maybe the kid could give us information that would save me time in my search for Ben.

We hurried in to question him, but his mumblings made no sense. He kept drifting in and out of consciousness. The only clue he gave us was during his delirium. He sat upright in bed and stared at the wall, saying, "Don't, Rafe. No more. Don't hit the man no more."

Back in the kitchen, Joe said, "That don't mean anything. How do we know he's talking about Ben?"

"We don't, but would you be willing to give odds that he *wasn't* talking about Ben?"

Joe shook his head. "You know, he might be dead."

"No. If he was, then why was that yahoo in there still hanging around this part of the country?"

Joe considered the question. "If they haven't killed him, then what's their game?"

That was the question I had been turning over in my head the entire trip from my ranch back to the Eastlands'. What were Cutler and his bunch up to? It puzzled me. "Figure it this way," I said. "Ben appears to be a right smart businessman. Well, this man who's trying to get the contract away from Ben must be smart too. A hardscrabble cowpoke like me or you sure don't know anything about rich freight contracts."

Joe frowned. "I don't get what you're trying to say."

I leaned forward. "Just this. This Jordan fella's bound to be looking down the road and trying to anticipate what might happen. You want a rich contract. You don't mind wading a bunch of creeks or jumping a twelve-foot fence for it, but you figure that if you kill someone over it, then more likely than not the law will catch up with you sooner or later. Right?"

"Okay. So what?"

"A smart man doesn't like that kind of odds. All Jordan's got to do is stall Ben Ross so it will look like Jordan's the only one interested in the contract. Once he has it, he turns Ben loose. What can Ben do?"

Joe nodded. "I follow you. Then folks would just reckon he was bellyaching." He paused. "Of course, you're just supposing."

I looked him square in the eye. "I know, and I could be wrong." I nodded to the front porch, where Jodie was sitting on the swing with Mercy. "Chances of my finding him are a lot better if we can make her stay here. There's no way I can do what needs to be done if I got to worry about her. Besides, like I told you, Cutler's tried to take her once. He'll try again. She needs to stay here so you can keep an eye on her."

Joe clucked sympathetically. "I'll try."

He succeeded, and, thoroughly provisioned, I rode out early next morning after Jodie swore that she would remain at the Eastlands'. She had learned her lesson about running off across the prairie by herself.

Late that afternoon, I spotted the Red. I had decided to spend the night in the cave. Dusk was thickening by the time I reached it. After a light meal, I turned down the lantern and slipped outside. Taking care to skirt the nest of rattlesnakes, I climbed up to the bluffs overlooking the Red. I hadn't expected to see anything, so I wasn't disappointed. But just as I turned back to the cave, I heard the muffled report of a gunshot to the east. Hurrying back to the edge of the bluff, I peered into the darkness, but I neither saw nor heard anything.

Still, the shot boosted my hopes. The odds were that one of Cutler's gang had discharged the gun. If it was Cutler's bunch, sooner or later, one of them had to move around, for restless, on-the-go yahoos can't tolerate the boredom of a long camp.

The next morning before sunup, I eased to the top of the bluffs and lay on my belly so I could get a good view of the Red both east and west of me. The sun rose, and the stone began to warm up.

To the west, a coyote zigzagged across the sandy riverbed in pursuit of a tiny animal. Birds circled overhead. Once, a hawk swooped, pursued by a handful of darting sparrows.

By midmorning, I had grown mighty uncomfortable sprawled out on top of that bluff. The sun had baked me just as it had baked the sandstone. I slid backward until I could stand without being spotted from below and returned to the cool of the cave.

I spent the afternoon in a cave fronting the river. It was cool, and I had a fair view despite the willow brakes lining the bank. If I didn't spot anyone or anything today, I would move down the river.

The afternoon dragged on. In the distance, heat rose from the prairie, contorting the landscape into wavy patterns. Just before dusk, I rose to head back to my cave, disgusted and frustrated. Before I stepped outside, I heard the scrape of a horseshoe on the sandstone plate.

I pressed up against the wall of the cave and drew my gun. The soft shuffling grew closer. Moments later, a vaquero wearing a broad sombrero with a gaudy band of silvery material around the brim rode into sight, his body relaxed and rolling with the slow stride of his horse. He had a rifle lying across his saddle horn.

I cocked my revolver. "Hold it right there," I said.

He froze. His horse sidestepped once or twice.

"Drop the rifle and climb down — this side."

"*Sí*, I do as you say, señor. Do not shoot. I have no money."

"Tie your horse to the willow, and move slow. I've got this Colt lined up right in the middle of your back."

He did exactly as he was told. When he turned around, he recognized me. His eyes grew wide, but just as quickly he tried to cover his surprise. I motioned him into the cave, where I tied his hands behind him.

He seemed to be a few years older than me, maybe around thirty-four or thirty-five. His face was brown, and his hair was as black as the inside of the cave. He wore typical caballero attire, the *chaqueta* and the flashy *calzónes* split from hip to ankle, although both jacket and pantaloons had seen better days and were in dire need of a good scrubbing.

"Where's Ben Ross?" I demanded.

A faint grin curled one side of his lips. "Who is Ben Ross, señor? I am not from around here."

"Stop playing games. You know who I am. You were in Cutler's camp the other night."

He shrugged. "I know of no one by the name of Cutler, señor. As I said, I am not from this country. I am just traveling through, hoping to find work."

I studied him silently, the amused look in his eyes, the half grin on his lips. We both knew he was lying, and we both knew that he would continue to lie.

But then I had an idea. "One more chance. Where's Ben Ross?"

He glanced at the muzzle of my Colt, then shrugged.

"Turn around."

He did as I said. I blindfolded him, then led him out to his horse. Hoisting him into the saddle I led the horse and rider back to my cave.

Once inside, I lit the lantern, stuffed a bag in my pocket, pulled the vaquero from the saddle, grabbed my lariat, and led the outlaw deeper into the cave. He would tell me exactly what I wanted to know.

With each step, I felt the muscles in his arm grow more tense. I led him into the great chamber. "Sit," I said, positioning the blindfolded vaquero against one of the stubbing posts for the rope bridge and tying him securely.

I left him in the darkness and made my way back to the rattlesnake nest. Ten minutes later, I stopped in front of the den and set the lantern down. I had gone back to the river and cut down a small willow, its diameter about the size of my wrist. I lopped off all its limbs except one at the bottom, which I left three inches long to form a hook.

I inserted the willow into the den. When I felt it touch the rattlers, I twisted it several times, hoping to hook one of the snakes and curl it around the willow. As a boy back in Tennessee, I had used the same trick.

It worked better than I remembered. I pulled out three angry snakes. Quickly they separated and headed back for the den. I grabbed the largest by the tail and swung him away from the rocks, where I pressed the end of the willow against his neck, pinning his head to the ground.

Then I dropped him into the bag I had jammed in my pocket.

Back in the chamber, I removed the blindfold and set the lantern on the floor in front of the sullen vaquero. I tossed the willow branch behind me. "You ready to tell me what I want to know?" I dangled the bag in front of him.

He tried not to appear curious, but his eyes betrayed him as he kept glancing at the bag. "I know nothing, señor."

I jiggled the bag. "You're certain?"

"*Sí*. As I said, I was passing through, looking for work."

"Have it your own way." Using the toe of my boot, I kicked his feet apart and scooted the lantern between them.

Stepping back several feet, I knelt on the floor and laid the bag in front of me. I nodded at the lantern. "I know it's hot, amigo, but I want you to have plenty of light so you can see what's going to happen to you."

His Adam's apple bobbed like a cork. Sweat glistened on his face, but he kept his lips pressed together tightly. The yellow glow from the lantern revealed the fear in his eyes.

Slowly, I untied the bag and gently slid the coiled rattler onto the smooth floor. The Mexican sucked in his breath.

I stepped back, my hand near my .44. I knew I couldn't let the snake strike the vaquero, regardless of what he had done, but I hoped I could scare him enough to tell me what I wanted to know before I had to kill the snake.

As soon as the rattler saw the lantern, it coiled and faced the light. Its deadly song filled the room, a steady hum that vibrated the smooth floor at my feet. The vaquero stiffened.

"What do you say now, amigo? Do you want to tell me where you have Ben Ross?"

He was mumbling under his breath, and perspiration beaded his forehead.

The rattler arched its neck, and its tongue tested the air. The serpent made one or two tentative strikes at the lantern. The Mexican blubbered.

"Where are you keeping Ben Ross?"

He looked at me. "Señor, I tell you truly. I do not know of whom you speak. I —"

Using the willow, I prodded the rattler. It struck the branch instantly and uncoiled. For several seconds, it looked into the darkness, then slowly curled back on itself and glided toward the lantern.

A scream tore from the vaquero's throat.

"Ben Ross. Is he alive?"

He didn't answer.

The rattlesnake drew closer to the lantern.

I unleathered my gun and stepped to the side so the ricochet wouldn't hit the man. "You heard me. Is he alive? Answer me, or I'll feed you to the snake."

"*Sí*, señor, *sí*, he is alive."

Moving quickly, I stepped forward and grabbed the snake's tail and swung him away from the vaquero. "Where?"

He shook his head.

Pinning the snake, I grabbed it behind the head and squatted in front of the prone man, who drew back against the post. I held the serpent inches from his face. "Amigo, you have five seconds to tell me what I want to hear." I squeezed the rattler's neck; it opened its mouth. The long curved fangs shone in the pale light. Golden drops of venom oozed from their needle points.

He began to cry. "I tell you! I tell you, señor!"

I kept the snake in his face. "Where is he?"

"Downriver — in a cave."

"Which one? How do I recognize it?"

For a moment, he remained silent. I pushed the rattler closer. He screamed. "A great red boulder sits before it, guarding the mouth of the cave."

"How many men does Cutler have?"

"Three — four, counting himself. *Por favor,* señor, I beg you. Do not kill me. I do not go back to Cutler. I leave Texas — back to Sonora from where I come."

"What's your part in all this?"

He shook his head, his eyes wide with fear. "I do not know, señor. Mr. Cutler, he hire us. He just say he will pay each a hundred pesos if we help."

Satisfied that I had learned all I could, I dropped the rattler back in the bag, untied the vaquero, and blindfolded him again. Outside, I turned the rattler loose in front of its den.

The next morning, back at the Red, I removed the blindfold from the vaquero. That's when I saw that his hair had turned as white as snow. His dark eyes moved unceasingly, darting about like a frightened and injured bird trying to avoid the rattlesnake. His body trembled. I removed the cartridges from his revolver and tossed it to him.

"Get out of the country. If I catch you again, you know what will happen."

He nodded and yanked his horse west, digging his sharp rowels into the animal's flanks in the same motion.

I watched him cross the Red and cut south across the prairie. Within minutes, the short grass and sagebrush had swallowed him. Now I had to take care of Cutler.

That evening, just before dark, a bank of clouds swept in from the southwest, bringing a fine mist with them. I couldn't believe my luck. Inclement weather would keep Cutler's sentries from casting about too far. If my luck and the bad weather continued, I would be able to slip in close to the cave, perhaps close enough to spirit Ben away from them.

I moved down into the willow brakes and headed downriver, trusting that I could spot both their horses and their fire before they saw me. Thirty minutes later, I spied orange shadows dancing on the interior walls of a cave. But I saw no horses, unless. . . . I dropped to my knees and peered through the willows.

Sure enough, a large boulder appeared in silhouette before the fire. I had found the cave.

Drawing my Colt, I slipped forward, straining my eyes to penetrate the darkness. I studied every shadow, every stump, not once but several times, hoping to spot the sentry before he saw me.

The fine mist thickened. Despite the season, the mist chilled me. It must have chilled the sentry too and driven him inside to the fire, because he was nowhere outside. I crept forward, seeking a refuge from which I could see inside the cave. Finally I found a small copse of young willows that allowed me to peer into the cave without being seen.

The tiny fire gave off enough light so that I could make out a single vaquero facing the fire. He cupped a tin mug in his hands and blew on it.

A worry nagged at me. He appeared to be by himself, except for a single, inert figure on the floor beyond the fire. What had happened to the others? Were they back in the cave sleeping? No — they would be sleeping by the fire just like the other one. So where had they gone?

Settling back against a willow, I watched the cave. After the lone sentry finished his coffee, he rose, stretched, then moved to the cave entrance where he pulled out his revolver and spun the cylinder half a dozen times. He holstered his firearm and sauntered back into the cave to stand over the figure on the floor.

A few minutes later, he disappeared into the darkness of the cave. A soft whinny sounded from the darkness. I grinned to myself — I had been right about where they had put their horses.

Moving silently, I slipped through the willows until I was only a few feet from the boulder. Rising to a crouch, I dashed across the small clearing to it. Suddenly, I heard the crunch of boots on sand from within the cave. The steps paused. In my mind's eye, I could see the vaquero standing in the mouth of the cave, studying the night.

He yawned and stepped out of the cave onto the sandstone plate at our feet. The steps grew louder. I backed around the boulder, keeping my Colt facing the sound of his oncoming steps. He stopped in front of the boulder.

I glanced over my shoulder. The mouth of the cave was less than ten feet away. Squatting, I picked up a small stone and hurled it into the willows.

"What!" the guard exclaimed.

When he stepped forward to investigate the source of the sound, I slipped into the cave and hid in the darkness in the rear. I glanced at the inert figure as I passed. His face was hidden by shadows, but I knew it was Ben Ross because of the firelight flickering across his brogans.

Soon the sentry returned. With his back to me, he squatted by the fire and reached for a cup and the coffeepot. As soon as his hands were full, I stepped forward and jammed the muzzle of my revolver in his back. "Don't move a muscle," I ordered.

He went rigid.

I leaned forward and slipped his revolver from the holster. "Lie down and put your hands behind your back."

He did as told. Quickly I tied, gagged, and blindfolded him. Then I pulled a burning branch from the fire and slipped into the darkness to the rear of the cave. Only one horse stood in the makeshift rope corral. Holstering my .44, I didn't pause to consider the situation. My only thought was to spirit Ben away.

He was unconscious. A dirty strip of muslin was wrapped around his chest, darkly stained just below his right shoulder. After cutting his bonds, I heaved him on the horse and hurriedly lashed him to the saddle. He groaned and winced when I jarred his shoulder. "Can you hear me, Ben?" I whispered.

He moaned and opened his eyes and stared at me. They were glazed with pain. "Jodie? Is that you, Jodie?"

Without hesitation, I led the horse from the cave.

Minutes later, I reached my cave, where I lashed Ben to Joe Eastland's horse and mounted the vaquero's. We had some hard riding to do, and I didn't want to take a chance on a green horse throwing Ben. Joe's horse was the same gentle mare Ross had borrowed when he had first headed out for Fort Worth.

At midmorning, the Eastland ranch came into view. I looked over my shoulder at Ben. A bright crimson circle enveloped the older, darker stain. His wound had opened. *Just a few more minutes,* I told myself, urging my horse across the prairie.

The thought of a hot bath and a solid, rib-sticking meal brought a grin to my face. Ben could rest up, and then we would head for Fort Worth. Dreams of the grand ranch I would build came rushing back.

Joe Eastland, followed by his entire family, came hurrying from the ranch house as I rode up. I knew something was wrong from the expression on his face.

"Matt — Cutler got her. Jodie's gone!"

Chapter Ten

While we put Ben to bed, Joe told me that Cutler's men had caught Jodie when she went to the barn.

"The barn? What was she doing out there?"

Joe handed me a note. "Feeding her horse, I reckon." He led the way to the kitchen, where Martha set a fat slice of steak between two steaming slabs of fresh homemade bread in front of me. I sent Michael out to saddle a fresh horse while I ate. I had to move out of there quickly.

Mercy came in and poured me a cup of coffee while I read the kidnapper's note. "Insurance? They want her for insurance?" I looked up at Joe. "Just how do you figure that kind of logic? They had Ben, and I don't reckon they figured anyone would try to rescue him. Why did they figure they needed more insurance?"

Joe shrugged. "Hard to figure them kind of outlaws. Maybe Cutler had a hunch."

"Maybe, but if that's what he acted on, he sure got lucky." I reread the note. The kidnappers promised to turn Jodie and Ben loose as soon as they were satisfied that the deal was set in Fort Worth. "What do you figure they'll do when they get back and find Ben gone?" I sipped my coffee. Martha had made it strong enough to straighten horseshoes.

"I don't know, but whatever it is, you'd better head back," Joe answered. He paused and glanced over his shoulder, then lowered his voice. "But I got some more bad news, Matt. Some that is goin' to be mighty painful for you."

I eyed Joe warily. I'd come close to having my fill of bad news. "What is it?"

"Banker Simmons came out. You got to bring the mortgage up to date by this time next month, or he's goin' to start foreclosing procedures on you."

The announcement knocked the breath out of me. "But he gave me a year. That won't be up for another nine months," I said, astonished.

Joe shrugged. "He said the board overrode him."

For several seconds, I struggled to sort my priorities. I had to go after Jodie, but there was no way I could let myself lose the ranch, not the ranch my father and mother and sister had died defending.

Joe leaned across the table. "You all right, Matt?"

I stared at him, then nodded to the bedroom

where Ben lay. "Look, Joe. I've got to get back out there and find Jodie. Do me a favor and go see Simmons. Explain to him that Ben is going to advance me enough to bring the note up to date."

"I told him. He said fine, but he would have to see the money first."

I blew through my lips slowly. "That's all I can do, then." I refused to let myself believe that I might fail. I told myself that as soon as I got Jodie back and Ben was up and out of bed, we'd go into town and bring the note up to date.

"You know if I had the money, Matt, I'd be mighty glad to make you a loan," Joe said.

"I know, Joe. Thanks."

"But there is some good news," he said. "Many Dogs rode in early this morning. He brought in your horse and Jodie's. Said he found them wandering out on the prairie." He paused, then added, a big grin on his face, "He said that might make up for a little of what happened out there in the canyon."

I smiled. "He's a good friend."

Socks was back — that *was* good news. Then I remembered Billy Wayne. Joe said he was doing well and improving every day.

"In fact," Joe said with a wink, "I reckon you done lost an admirer. That daughter of mine stays by the boy's side every minute.

I don't reckon she would ever forgive him if he didn't get well."

"What kind of kid is he?" I asked. "He seemed to be pretty much the innocent out there."

Joe grunted. "That's the way it appears. Accordin' to him, he'd been with Cutler only a few days when they rode in here that day. Cutler offered him a job, and he figured, 'why not.' "

"And so Mercy dotes on him now, huh?"

An amused smile split Joe's angular face. "And then some."

I grinned, but deep inside, I felt a touch of envy — and sadness. Everyone likes to be thought of as someone special. And secretly I liked that feeling myself, knowing that little Mercy felt that way about me, but now. . . . Well, I was glad for Mercy, for I had always liked her as a sister, nothing else. And I would never want to see her hurt. Let her think that Billy Wayne was someone special. I hoped for her sake that he was.

Martha gave me my parfleche bag filled with grub. Joe walked outside with me. Michael stood at the hitching rail with Socks. I took the reins and patted my horse on the neck. "You don't look any worse for wear."

"Looks like Many Dogs took good care of him for you."

Mounting, I nodded. "He did a fine job."

Joe laid his hand on the reins. His face was serious. "Be careful, Matt."

I forced an unfelt grin. "You know me, Joe. Careful's my middle name."

I reached the river after dark and threaded my way through the boulders and underbrush to my cave. After unsaddling and graining Socks, I slipped into the night, hoping that Cutler had not switched his camp to another cave.

Easing through the willow brakes, I studied the area ahead of me, keeping my eyes constantly moving, never focusing, but gazing, using my peripheral vision in the darkness. Abruptly I halted. I saw movement within the dark mass of the willow brakes. I dropped to one knee behind a willow and studied the darkness.

A horse whinnied. I shook my head with a sense of reluctant admiration — Cutler was nobody's fool. The movement within the brakes was being made by their remuda. He had ordered the horses corralled outside the cave.

Now, I told myself, not only did I have to keep an eye out for the sentry but I also had to be sure the horses didn't catch my scent. An unfamiliar smell could spook them.

The light wind was from the east, so for the time being I was safe. But the bluffs did crazy things with the wind, causing it to spiral and curl. At any moment, the breeze could shift, carrying my scent to the horses.

Slowly, I backed away. I had to get closer, but how? Any strange smell would alarm the horses. If I couldn't reach the cave, the only solution was to bring the cave to me — or at least the sentry.

I returned to the cave for some rope and my lariat, which I threw over a slender willow. Using another tree as a pulley for leverage, I bent the willow to the ground and notched it down. I laid out a loop of rope and covered it with a thin layer of sand. Another rope served as the trigger. Then I backed off a few feet and lay down on the ground. I drew the trigger rope taut.

A gust of wind peppered my face with sand. As soon as the wind let up, I gave a loud groan.

One of the horses whinnied.

I waited several seconds, then moaned again.

A guttural voice steadied the horses. Then there was silence.

Once again I moaned.

Footsteps in the sand came toward me, a scratching, crunching sound, but the sentry was lost in the bulk of darkness in the willow brake. Then the footsteps stopped. I held my breath and strained my ears.

The sound began again. Suddenly, the silhouette of a man's head and shoulders appeared above the dark background. It was one of the vaqueros. He halted.

I lay less than twenty feet from him. I gave a soft moan.

His head turned toward me. For several seconds, he remained motionless, then he took a step. I knew what he saw, how I appeared to him: a dark object like a log on the sand.

He drew closer.

Then I yanked the rope.

The notch flew off and the willow shot upright, whipping the vaquero's feet out from under him before he had a chance to utter a word. Instantly, I leaped to my feet and grabbed his swinging body and jammed the muzzle of my .44 in his mouth.

"One sound, amigo, and buzzards will be picking your bones."

He nodded.

I slipped his jacket off and tied his hands. Quickly I finished binding and gagging him and then dragged him to a nearby cave. After donning his jacket and sombrero, I sauntered lazily toward the horses.

One or two snorted, but they recognized the vaquero's scent and remained calm. I paused in the darkness in the willow brakes and peered into the cave.

A vaquero and the man named Two-Bit lay with their heads on their saddles on either side of the fire. Beyond them sat Jodie. She was leaning against the cave wall, and her hands were tied in front of her. A rope was strung from her wrists to one of the saddles. Her chin rested on her chest. Above her, a lantern burned dimly. Cutler was nowhere in sight. I breathed a sigh of relief. She appeared unhurt.

I went back to the horses. There were only three. I stared into the darkness surrounding me. Cutler was out there somewhere, maybe approaching the camp even as I waited.

I considered the situation. A gunfight was out of the question. Jodie might catch a stray slug. If only there were some way to scare them. If —

Suddenly, I had an idea, a risky, crazy one, but if it worked, if I could complete it before Cutler returned, if I were lucky. . . .

I hurried back to the cave and retrieved the willow I had used to catch the rattlesnake. I dumped the grub from the parfleche bag and grabbed the lantern. The light would be risky, but to do what I planned would be insane in the dark.

I stopped at the rattlesnake den and pulled

another snake from the hole. He was a large one, about the size of my arm. Quickly I dropped him into the bag, snugged down the thongs on the flap, and turned out the lantern.

Then I hurried back to Cutler's cave, pausing to count the horses. There were still only three.

As I drew closer to the cave, voices reached my ears. I halted in the brake and peered through the willows. Two-Bit was propped up on his elbow and speaking to the vaquero, but I was too far away to hear. After a moment, he lay down and turned his back on the Mexican.

I looked at the parfleche bag in my hand. I had the snake. Now, how was I going to get it in the cave without being spotted?

Backtracking, I tied a loop in a thong on the parfleche bag. I cut another willow limb, and moved into the shadows along the bluffs. The only way they could see me would be if they stuck their heads outside and peered up into the shadows. I moved along the bluff to a few feet away from the cave entrance, stuck the end of the limb through the loop in the thong, and quietly lowered the bag just inside the mouth of the cave.

Leaving the sleeping men with their surprise, I threw the other vaquero over my shoulder and carried him to another cave farther upriver. I would come back for him later. There were only three outlaws left now, and with any luck, tomorrow there would be only two.

I spent the remainder of the night hiding in the brakes, close enough to keep an eye on the cave, and far enough that Cutler wouldn't stumble across me if he decided to put in an appearance.

The outlaw rode in just before sunrise. Cutler reined his sorrel to a halt and looked around before dismounting. He gave his head a disgusted shake when he failed to see a lookout.

Inside the cave, the fire had burned low, and the two outlaws slumbered peacefully. I could barely make out the bundled figure on the floor behind them. The parfleche bag remained on the floor by the wall where I had set it.

Cutler dismounted and strode into the cave, almost kicking over the parfleche bag. Instead, he kicked the vaquero in the back. "Get up, you lazy galoot. Who's supposed to be out there looking after things?" When the Mexican sat up, Cutler demanded, "Where's Luis?"

The sleep-drugged vaquero stumbled to his feet and tried to shake the fatigue from his eyes. He nodded to the horses. "There."

Jodie sat up, frightened by the loud tirade.

"No, he ain't," Cutler roared.

The second outlaw had awakened by now.

Cutler turned on him. "Where's Luis, Two-Bit?"

Two-Bit jumped to his feet and shook his head. "I don't know, Rafe. He was supposed to wake me around three to take the watch." The outlaw kept a wary eye on Cutler, who seemed on the verge of blowing up. "I'll go look, Rafe. He mighta just took a walk down the river." Two-Bit grabbed his hat and jammed it on his head, and, deliberately skirting Cutler, scurried toward the entrance.

Two-Bit hesitated at the entrance. "What's this?" He stared down at the parfleche bag, then glanced back at Cutler.

Cutler replied, his tone well laced with sarcasm, "Who knows what it is, with you two around? Maybe a pack rat stole Luis and left you a present."

Two-Bit gave an uncomfortable laugh as he squatted and reached for the parfleche bag. He opened it and lowered his head to look inside.

A blur shot from the bag, and Two-Bit's scream cut through the brittle silence of early morning. "I'm bit! He got me! I'm snakebit!"

What little remained of the early-morning tranquillity was quickly dispatched by two gunshots as the vaquero fired at the rattlesnake, which was slithering back into the cave. He missed.

Cutler shoved him aside with a burly forearm. The big man moved with deceptive speed. His hand shot out and grabbed the rattlesnake by the tail and swung the reptile over his head like he was roping a cow and neatly popped the snake's head off. Then the sneering outlaw tossed the serpent's thrashing body at the feet of the vaquero.

Two-Bit had run outside holding the side of his neck. He dropped to his knees. Deep, drawn-out moans came from his lips.

Inside, Cutler calmly stirred up the fire and put coffee on to boil. The vaquero stood uncertainly, looking first at Two-Bit, then back at Cutler. "I reckon that'll teach you to tie your gear up tight. Rattlers are always looking for a quiet home," Cutler said.

Jodie stood behind Cutler, her hands pressed against her lips. Cutler finally noticed her. He stood and looked around the cave. His face darkened, and he turned to the vaquero. "Where's Ross?"

The vaquero took a step back. He shrugged. "He is not here, Señor Cutler. When Señor Two-Bit and I came back with the señorita, we find Luis tied and with a blindfold. He did not see who took Ross."

Cutler drew back his arm and took a threatening step toward the vaquero. He stopped and glared at the frightened Mexican. "Can't you do anything right?" He shook his head in disgust and turned back to the fire, angrily throwing more wood on it.

Outside, Two-Bit toppled over on his side. His body shivered, stiffened, then went limp.

I took a deep breath and tried to still the pounding in my chest. Cocking the hammer of my .44, I eased forward. There would never be a better time to take care of Cutler.

The two outlaws had their backs to me as I slipped forward. I was concentrating so hard on what I was doing that I didn't hear Luis come up behind me. In my haste, I must have been careless with his bonds. He had gotten free. Suddenly, the cold muzzle of a handgun jammed into my spine. "Do not move, señor."

I froze. Luis reached around me and took my Colt.

Cutler spun, his own revolver leaping into his hand as if by magic. When he saw me, his face grew hard. "I had a gut feeling you was mixed up in all this somehow. And now everything kinda falls into place. One of my boys missing, two dead, Ross gone — and you poppin' up all over the place."

He swaggered over to me and stuck his nose in my face. His breath was rancid with stale smoke and cheap whiskey. "Yeah, mister, I'd say you caused me a right bit of trouble."

"Not as much as I wished I could have." I glared back at him, every muscle in my body tense.

He sneered and turned back to the fire. I relaxed. Suddenly he spun and threw a right hook at me. I saw it coming, but I couldn't react in time. Stars exploded in my skull, and I felt myself falling into a deep, dark well.

I awakened later, hog-tied and dizzy. My head throbbed, and my jaw ached.

"Are you okay?"

Jodie's voice cut through the fog swirling in my skull. I didn't answer at first. Then I felt her shoulder touch mine. "I guess so," I mumbled, having some difficulty saying the words. "What about you?"

"They haven't hurt me." She hesitated. She spoke again, and this time concern filled her voice. "Are you sure you're all right?"

I nodded, and my head exploded. I closed my eyes against the throbbing pain and held my head motionless in a fruitless effort to still the agony.

"Is my father okay?"

"Bullet wound," I whispered, trying not to move any part of my body I didn't have to.

She gasped.

"Not serious," I said. "He'll be fine."

Rafe Cutler's deep voice boomed across the cave. "Well, look who decided to join the living." He paused to pour some whiskey into his coffee and then came over to stand at my feet.

Behind him, Luis glared at me. The other vaquero was outside. Cutler tapped the bottom of my foot with the toe of his boot. He grinned wickedly when I looked up at him. "Yeah, you caused me some trouble. Now, I got to decide what to do with you."

I remained silent. Jodie started to speak up, but I hushed her.

Cutler laughed, a sneering, mocking laugh. "The gent's right in shushing you, lady. Nothing you can say will change my mind. 'Course, I ain't rightly decided just what I will do with you two, but whatever it is, you can bank on it being mighty special." He took a deep drink of his coffee and whiskey. "I could turn you loose. Ain't no real reason to hold you now that Ross lost the freight contract."

I looked up at him just as Jodie gasped out, "What did you say?"

He laughed again and drained his coffee. He went back to the fire and picked up his whiskey bottle and came back to us. He turned up the bottle and filled his cup full of rotgut. "Yep. Old Ben Ross lost the contract. I got word yesterday that Mr. Arnold J. Jordan signed the contract a couple of days back. Seems like," he added, mocking us, "for some reason Ben Ross just didn't want the contract bad enough to travel all the way to Fort Worth for it. It's a shame, but then some men just don't want to work that hard."

"You . . . you. . . ." Jodie sputtered in her anger.

Cutler laughed again.

"Then you got what you want. Let us go," I said.

He shook his head. "Nope. Not yet. I got me some thinking to do on it. You see, the way I figure it is that the law might believe three of you were kidnapped, but if you two was to disappear, then it would be old Ben Ross's word against mine." He took another big drink from his cup.

"You're forgetting the note," I said.

He frowned at me. "What note?"

"The one your men left when they took Jodie. They said they wanted her for insurance. You can bet the law will pay attention to something like that."

His face darkened. Turning on his heel, he went back to the fire.

"What's he going to do to us?" Jodie whispered.

"I don't know. All we can do is wait and watch." I tried to sound confident, but I

156

wasn't. We had to do something, but my brain just wouldn't function.

The outlaw's revelation about the contract had driven an icy knife in my chest. If Ben lost the contract, then he couldn't hire me. That meant no money for the mortgage. And Wentworth sure wouldn't lend me money. He had made that plain. Despair plopped down on my shoulders like a three-hundred-pound hog. Everything my family and I had worked for had gone up like a prairie fire.

I tried to push aside my disappointment about the ranch. If we didn't get out of here, a ranch wouldn't make any difference.

I began to work on the rawhide binding my wrists while Cutler sat by the fire and continued working on his bottle. Both vaqueros were outside, working at staying away from Cutler.

From the angle of the sun, nighttime was only a couple of hours away. I figured that we had tonight, and that was it. If we were lucky, Cutler would drink himself into a stupor. If not. . . . I kept sawing at my bonds, not wanting to think about the alternative.

By dusk, Cutler was snoring by the fire, cradling the empty bottle in his arm. The vaqueros huddled together, whispering and throwing surly glances at the sleeping outlaw and occasionally at us. I had worked steadily on the rawhide bonds, sawing them on the sandstone at my back, halting whenever one of the Mexicans looked at us. The bonds were beginning to stretch as the soft stone cut slowly into the rawhide.

Sweat beaded on my forehead, and Jodie noticed. "What if they see the perspiration on your face? They'll think you're up to something."

"Maybe," I whispered. "Let's hope they stay where they are. I got a feeling those two are looking for a way out of here just like we are."

The fire burned low. The vaqueros rose to their feet. I held my breath. Luis rolled up in his bedroll while the other vaquero went outside for his watch. Neither thought to light the lantern over our head. I sawed frantically at the rawhide. The scraping sound seemed to fill the silent cave, but Cutler and Luis continued their snoring.

I lost track of time, but it must have been well after midnight when the rawhide snapped in two. I waited and listened. Satisfied that the two men still slept, I untied my feet and quickly freed Jodie. She headed for the cave entrance, but I laid my hand on her arm.

"This way," I whispered, nodding to the rear of the cave.

Then a footstep sounded from the front of

the cave. Immediately, we sat back and pretended we were sleeping. The vaquero stared down at us for several long seconds, then shuffled back to the fire and awakened Luis. He grumbled but went outside for his turn at watch.

We waited. An hour passed, and the vaquero snored blissfully. "Let's go," I whispered. I lifted the lantern off its hook and led the way deeper into the cave. "Hold on to my belt. I've got to feel our way until we can light the lantern."

I moved slowly, reaching out with my toe at each step, for I remembered the hole in the middle of the tunnel in the first cave. The floor of the cave was soft. I didn't tell Jodie, but if Cutler decided to look back in the tunnel for us, he would have no trouble picking up our tracks. Several yards past the first bend, I lit the lantern, keeping it in front of me to prevent light from spilling back into the room where Cutler slept.

We hurried forward.

"Why did we come this way?" Jodie asked.

"The guard outside. He might have spotted us. Besides, that's what their first thought will be, that we slipped outside."

She didn't reply. We kept moving quickly in the general direction of the first cave, remembering Joe's statement that all of these caves were connected. If we could reach the first cave, then we could go out the rear entrance where my horse was picketed, even if we had to cross the rope bridge again.

The cave twisted and turned, but I tried to keep heading west, although there were times I wasn't sure which direction was which.

An hour later, the cave opened into a large room. To our left, the gray of dawn shone through the mouth of the cave. I held the lantern over my head. The room looked familiar.

I turned back to Jodie with a big grin on my face. "This is it. This is the cave we were looking for."

The weariness fled her face. She smiled broadly. "Then we're safe. We got away from Cutler."

A sarcastic voice cut through the darkness. "Not quite, little lady. Not quite." The crisp click of a hammer being cocked put a final punctuation mark to the words.

I turned to the voice, and Rafe Cutler stepped into the light, a sneer on his lips.

Chapter Eleven

"When I saw your tracks, I figured this was what you had in mind," Cutler said. "Pity that you weren't smart enough to figure that there could be others who knew about these caves."

I looked past him for the vaqueros. He laughed. "They'll be here directly. I got 'em watching a couple other places where the cave comes out," he said, almost eager to let me know just how familiar he was with the caves.

He gestured at the lantern with the muzzle of his handgun. "Set it down — easy."

I did as he said.

"Now turn around."

Again, I did as he ordered, looking for any chance to jump him before the vaqueros arrived.

Jodie gave me the chance. As Cutler stepped forward to bind my wrists, she yelled, "You leave him alone!" In the next breath, she threw herself at him, knocking him back and causing him to stumble over his own feet.

I spun and jumped at him just as he struck Jodie with the back of his hand, knocking her to the ground. I slammed my shoulder into his chest, driving him to the floor of the cave.

He was flat on his back with me astraddle. He swung a massive fist at my face. I jerked my head aside and smashed a fist into his jaw. The impact traveled all the way up to my shoulder, just as if I had slugged an iron plow.

From out of nowhere, his left fist caught me in the middle of my chest and sent me tumbling head over heels. Instantly, Cutler jumped to his feet and charged me. I rolled to my feet and sidestepped his rush, driving my fist into his kidney at the same time.

He grunted and spun around, throwing a roundhouse right that I managed to duck before slamming three fast blows into his rocky midsection. I backed away quickly, and a sweeping left glanced off my forehead. I stepped in behind his swing and threw a right cross that split the tightly drawn skin on his cheekbone.

He shook his head and charged again. This time I planted my feet and met him head-on. We stood toe-to-toe battering at each other. I tried to stay inside his massive arms, but his fists were like clubs beating on my arms and shoulders, slowly numbing them. He ducked his head and began bulling me back with a series of vicious uppercuts that slammed into my belly and chest. I worked my arms like pistons, hammering at his body.

No man grows up in Tennessee without fighting. So I had an abundance of experience, but fighting Rafe Cutler was like taking on a tree trunk. I didn't have his strength, but I was faster, which was my only advantage.

After a few seconds of standing toe-to-toe with him, I realized I was playing his game. The only way I could whip him was with my speed.

Abruptly, I stepped aside. Off balance, Cutler stumbled forward, and I drove a stiff left into the back of his head right behind his ear.

He roared with anger and charged again. This time, I stepped to the other side and grabbed his shirt and belt, and, using his forward momentum, slammed him into the side of the cave.

The outlaw's head bounced off the wall and he sprawled on the floor, momentarily stunned.

Just before I jumped on him, the two vaqueros appeared in the mouth of the cave. I grabbed the lantern and Jodie's hand. "This way," I yelled, heading back into the cave.

We raced down the tunnel, slowing as we skirted the hole in the floor. Once around the hole, we ran as fast as we could. Behind us came a jumble of voices, excited, angry, abusive. Then came the sounds of pursuit.

Cutler's grating voice echoed down the tunnel. "Slow down. There's —"

A scream cut him off, followed by more excited jabbering. I could only imagine what had happened. One of the vaqueros had raced ahead of the light and fallen into the hole.

We reached the first fork and turned right. When I realized we had taken the wrong turn, we had gone too far to turn back. Behind us, the footsteps grew louder. I glanced over my shoulder. I was right. The light behind us was growing brighter.

The cave forked again. We cut to the right, and the floor immediately began dropping at an angle so steep that we had to lean backward to keep from falling. Within minutes the steep descent moderated, although the tunnel continued to descend into the bowels of the earth.

Around one bend, the tunnel ran into water. I hesitated, but from behind came the sounds of pursuit. Taking Jodie's hand, I stepped into the water. It was only ankle-deep, and remained so for the next few hundred yards.

Abruptly the tunnel narrowed. I looked up. About ten feet above us was a ledge of some kind. I held the lantern up so the glow would illuminate the ceiling. A shadow cut along one side of the tunnel. There was indeed a ledge above, if only we could figure out how to reach it without leaving any sign.

"What's the matter?" Jodie whispered as I

continued studying the ledge.

"Up there. We could hide up there until they passed. Then we could slip out behind them. But," I added, "there's no way to get up there without dripping water on the rocks. That would be a sure giveaway." I pointed to the water we had splashed on the tunnel walls.

"That's it," Jodie exclaimed. "That's how we can fool them!"

I frowned at her. "What do you mean?"

"They can follow us by the water we splash on the walls, right?"

"That's right."

"Okay. Let's splash past the next fork for a hundred feet or so. You know, splash a lot of water on the side. Then we'll backtrack and head down the fork. We'll just have to be sure not to splash any water on those walls."

I saw exactly what she was suggesting, and it was a clever idea. Five minutes later, we came to the fork and did as she suggested, making sure to splash a lot of water on the tunnel walls. Then we backtracked and took the other fork, moving slowly and keeping our feet underwater so we wouldn't inadvertently leave sign.

The tunnel took a shallow bend. We stopped around the bend to wait. Minutes later, a pale light glowed in the far tunnel, then stopped at the fork. The men's voices carried clearly down the tunnel.

"Which way they go, Señor Cutler?"

"Straight ahead. Can't you see the water on the rocks?"

"Where this goes, señor?" The vaquero was frightened.

"I dunno. I never been down here. Water always spooked me. I've heard tell about drop-offs down in these waters that will suck you under."

The vaquero's teeth chattered.

Cutler pushed ahead. "Come on, amigo, unless you want to stay in the dark."

We waited until the glow from the lantern had disappeared, and then we lit our own lantern and headed back out. Fifteen minutes later, we waded out of the water and back-tracked out of the narrow cave into the main tunnel.

I held up the lantern to light our faces. Jodie's was smudged and weary. "Looks like we made it," I whispered.

Suddenly a shout echoed down the tunnel. "There's their light. Down there!"

I looked behind us. It couldn't be — unless the tunnel had curved back up into the main tunnel. But there he was. I could hear Cutler's guttural voice.

"Come on!" I shouted, taking Jodie's hand and racing down the tunnel. Around the next bend, I slid to a halt and held the lantern out to the wall. "Look." Cut into the wall of the cave was an alcove just like the one we had discovered in the other fork of the cave. And just as the other, there was a passage at the rear, which we took — but not in time to escape the notice of Cutler and the vaquero.

"In there!" Cutler yelled. "I see their light."

We ran down the hall and through a door that opened into a large room that appeared to have once housed an entire tribe of Indians. The blackened remains of ancient fires dotted the floor. Lances, bows, and war clubs lay scattered across the room, as if everyone had fled for their lives. On the outer edge of the lantern light, two totem poles stretched up into the darkness. They seemed be made out of the same kind of petrified rock as the snubbing posts in the other chamber.

The blast of a gunshot filled the room, deafening us. The slug exploded at the base of one of the totem poles, knocking a chunk of rock from the great column.

Cutler's harsh voice echoed through the chamber. "Hold it right there."

We halted.

Suddenly, a sharp crack cut through the silence, followed by a groan of straining rock.

There was another splintering crack, and out of the corner of my eye I saw the totem pole struck by the slug begin to topple. We spun just as Cutler yelled "Look out!" and jumped aside.

The vaquero screamed and dropped his light as the totem pole slammed to the floor. The lantern ruptured and exploded.

I looked at Cutler, who was scrabbling around searching for his handgun. "Cutler!"

He froze and slowly looked around at me. Something snapped in the man. I saw it as the blistering flames cast a blood-red glow on the frenzied fury twisting his bearded face. He jumped to his feet and looked around for some kind of weapon. Then he saw the lances on the floor. He grabbed one and charged me.

I stood   ground. At the last second, I sidestepped, letting the lance graze my side, and hooked my right fist into his throat. He dropped to his knees, clutching his throat, gagging. He was finished now.

Using the lantern, Jodie and I found his handgun. Just as we turned back, Cutler disappeared through another door.

Leaving Jodie in the chamber, I raced after Cutler. He wasn't going to escape punishment for what he had done. But as I ran out the door, the vaquero jumped me, knocking me to the floor and sending the handgun slithering across the hard rock floor.

We grappled, rolling over and over, fists flailing away at each other. The flames within the adjoining room cast an orange glow on us. I rolled to my feet and swung a solid right at the Mexican. I caught him on the chin and sent him sliding into the darkness.

Jodie stood in the doorway, silhouetted by the fire. "Matt!"

"I'm over here. Get the lantern." I stood on the edge of the soft glow, trying to peer into the surrounding darkness. "I can't see either of them."

Jodie came into the room with the lantern and gave it to me. Holding it ahead of me, I saw that we were in a huge chamber. The hair on the back of my neck prickled when I realized where we were. Quickly, I found the handgun, and holding it in one hand and the lantern in the other, started across the chamber.

A sick feeling churned in my stomach. Suddenly a guttural cry echoed through the darkness, followed by sobs.

I called into the darkness. "Cutler!"

A frightened cry came from beyond the glow of the lantern. I eased across the chamber in the direction of the cries. Suddenly, the light from the lantern fell across straining fingers clinging to the edge of the chasm, desperately struggling to claw into the hard, smooth floor. Sobs echoed from the darkness below. "Señor, *por favor,* help me, help me!"

Quickly I set the lantern down and reached for the vaquero's hands, but as I grabbed, he lost his grip and slipped into the darkness. My hands grasped nothing but air.

I lay motionless, my face pressed against the cold floor, listening, waiting for the impact of his hurtling body striking the bottom. But no sound reached my ears.

Holding the lantern over the edge, I peered into the darkness below. Within twenty feet, the darkness swallowed the light like water gulping down a rock.

And then I saw a narrow ledge about fifteen feet below the edge of the pit. It was well worn, and it appeared to be the threshold of a door. On the rim of the chasm, directly above the ledge, two holes were drilled in the floor about eighteen inches apart.

"What about Cutler?" Jodie asked.

I forgot about the ledge and stood up. He couldn't have gone far. We searched the large chamber and the smaller one next to it, but there was no sign of the outlaw leader.

"Maybe he fell into the pit too," Jodie said.

"Might have," I replied. "But I never heard him yell if he did."

Jodie smiled, then the smile faded. "Do you think Cutler lied when he said that Jordan had won the freight contract?"

"No, I think he told the truth." I paused. "I'm sorry for you and Ben. I know you were counting on it."

She laid her hand on mine. "You're the one who lost the most."

I had tried not to think about it, but she was right. No contract, no job. No job, no money. No money, no ranch. Yeah, I had lost a lot.

I felt her squeeze my hand. "Thank you for everything," she said softly.

I squeezed her hand back. "You're the one to thank." I touched her cheek, which was beginning to bruise. "You did a brave thing back there when you jumped him."

She blushed and laughed. It was a tinkling sound like crystal glass. "I just didn't want him to hurt you."

I took her hand again, and for several seconds, we stared into each other's eyes. Finally I grinned and said, "I guess we'd better go."

We searched the smaller chamber again, but there was no sign of the outlaw, although a few empty bottles and empty tomato cans strewn about indicated that the chamber had recently been used.

I picked up one of the lances. "Makes you wonder whose these were." Suddenly, I jerked to a halt, my eyes locked on a bunk that stretched the length of one wall. "That's strange," I muttered, noticing that the side-rails on one end of the bunk curved around like a fishhook.

We went closer. A few dirty and worn blankets lay on the bunk, which was about eighteen inches wide. Using the point of the lance, I removed the blankets.

"Why, that looks like a ladder of some kind," Jodie said.

She was right. Whoever had used this room as a refuge had utilized the ladder as a makeshift bed, an uncomfortable one, but it kept them off the floor and away from anything that might be crawling by.

But what intrigued me was the fishhook shape of the rails at one end of the ladder. Then I remembered the holes in the floor just above the ledge. Quickly I knelt and inspected the curved rails. They were round, about the size of the holes.

Giving Jodie the lantern, I leaned the ladder against the wall and quickly climbed it, jumping up and down on each of the rungs.

"What are you doing?"

"I'm not sure, but I think I know where this ladder goes."

"I don't understand."

"Just follow me." I shouldered the ladder and headed for the big chamber.

At the edge, I told Jodie about the ledge below the rim of the chasm and the holes in the floor. "I think this ladder fits in those holes. I don't know why, but if someone went to all the trouble to hide the entrance to a room this way, there must be something mighty important in it. Let's see." I lowered the ladder over the edge, and, as I thought, the curved ends of the rails slid precisely into the holes in the floor.

I removed my belt and looped it around the lantern handle. "Okay," I said. "Hold the lantern so I can see."

She lowered the lantern. "Be careful."

I climbed down the ladder and inspected the doorway. A slab door blocked the way. "Come on down," I said, climbing back up where I could take the lantern from her.

When Jodie reached the ledge, I gave her the lantern and threw my shoulder into the door. It opened with a creak as the bottom scraped across the rocky floor.

I took the lantern. Just before we stepped through the door, a guttural voice broke the darkness. "I got you! You'll never get out of here now!"

Cutler! We stepped back against the wall.

He kicked the ladder.

"Hold this," I shouted at Jodie as I grabbed for the ladder.

He kicked it free of the holes and toward the gaping pit. I grabbed it, straining to keep it from plunging into the darkness. He kicked at it again.

"Let go of it," he yelled. "You hear me, turn it loose." He kept kicking it as he said, "I told you to let it go. Let it —" Suddenly, he screamed and the ladder tore from my hands as he lost his balance and fell over the side into the darkness below. The ladder went with him.

"Dear God," Jodie breathed when I turned to face her. "How will we get out of here? I —" She began to cry.

I put my arm around her shoulders to still her shaking body. "We will. Don't worry," I said, taking the lantern. For several seconds, we remained motionless, staring into the darkness below us.

Finally, I said, "Well, let's see what's in here. Maybe we can find something to help us out of this mess." We stepped through the door and froze. The far wall reflected the glow of the lantern with a bright, yellow light of its own. "What —"

We both gaped in disbelief. Stacked against the wall were ingots of pure gold.

For several seconds, we could only stare at the gold, so bright and yellow, unable to absorb what our eyes were trying to tell us. Joe's stories were true after all.

"And look," I said, pointing to a ladder leaning against the wall. "Looks like whoever built this didn't want to take any chances on getting stuck down here."

Jodie looked up at me, and I grinned like a silly possum. "Maybe things are going to work out for us after all," I said.

She smiled mischievously. "For us?"

"Why not?" I asked, touching my fingers to her blond hair. "I got a feeling that this Panhandle gold is exactly what I've been looking for."

She laid her hand on mine. "And I think I've found what I've been looking for," she said, her eyes steady.

I gulped, then managed to choke out the words, "Then what are we going to do about it?"

She shrugged and asked innocently, "What do you suggest?"

Taking her hands in mine, I replied, "I think I'm going to talk to your father and see if he'd mind much if I took you off his hands. After all, twenty years is a long time for him to worry about you."

"Oh, and what about you? Will twenty years

be too much for you?"

I shook my head as I drew her close. "Twenty thousand isn't too much for me."